Redemption

Kay Langdale

W F HOWES LTD

This large print edition published in 2007 by
W F Howes Ltd
Unit 4, Rearsby Business Park, Gaddesby Lane,
Rearsby, Leicester LE7 4YH

1 3 5 7 9 10 8 6 4 2

First published in the United Kingdom in 2006
by Transita

The publisher would like to thank International
Creative Management Inc. for permission to reproduce
'Late Fragment' by Raymond Carver, from 'All of Us:
Collected Poems' (Harvill Press 1996)

A CIP catalogue record for this book is available
from the British Library

ISBN 978 1 40740 140 9

Typeset by Palimpsest Book Production Limited,
Grangemouth, Stirlingshire
Printed and bound in Great Britain
by Antony Rowe Ltd, Chippenham, Wilts.

Late Fragment

And did you get what
you wanted from this life, even so?
I did.
And what did you want?
To call myself beloved, to feel myself
beloved on the earth.

Raymond Carver

In memory of my grandmothers,
Florence Grace Langdale,
(1910–1971) and Winifred May Gilbert,
(1909–2001), strong women both.

CHAPTER 1

SARAH

Forsaking all others, keep thee only unto him

Sarah wondered, as she hung up the tea-towel, if her hands carried the faintest trace of the washing up gloves. Not how she would like to be perceived, she thought, forty-something and with an odour of damp rubber clinging to her fingertips. She was always mindful, as she examined a patient's eyes, that they were able to scrutinise her as closely as she could them. Each pore of the skin; the vagaries of the hair-line; the crumpling around the mouth; the bruised grey beneath the eye; a residue of milk in the corner of the lip from a cappuccino grabbed on the walk to work. How quickly, she knew, the intimate can become pedestrian. How quickly one loses all self-consciousness, close to a man's face, a woman's face, an old face, a child's face; looking deep behind the pupil at the spider's web of capillaries; looking for cataracts, for signs of glaucoma, all the time the patient's breath repetitive on her cheek.

The eyes as the window of the soul, there was a notion that could be quickly disabused. Instead, eyes

1

watery and red-rimmed from attempts to use contact lenses. Eyes that squinted, twitched, blinked shortsightedly at her charts. Sarah considered that her job had probably cured her of the inclination to look into someone's eyes as a gauge of personality, of veracity, of intent. No, eyes were too full of symptoms and contraindications for her; she looked elsewhere in the body for the clues that helped her piece together her sense of others. Perhaps this was why, recently, she kept her eyes closed when she had sex with Michael; kept her eyes shut, and thereby circumvented looking into his.

Sarah hadn't been to a wedding for years. Relatively recently a rash of christenings, and then nothing. If she saw a bride on the way to the village church, or saw the groom and ushers smoking a hasty cigarette by the porch, she was increasingly inclined to wonder how on earth they summoned the will to do it at all. How, at that stage, could people be so blind to the self-discipline, the self-sacrifice, that marriage exacted? Could they not anticipate how hard it was; how inappropriate it was to be preoccupied with the height of floral table centres, or the rear view of a dress, or a piece of music chosen to accompany the procession, when instead they should be focused on how they would look at this person for thirty years and not scream?

She thought of a friend who had casually joked about her husband, adding that *This of course was before I started hating him*. And they both laughed,

2

in a shared perception that she both did and did not hate him, and that such moments of intense resentment, of cold fury at being saddled with the same person, were entirely reasonable. So when she saw a bride, and thought of ribbon-tied boxes of sugared almonds given as bridal favours to guests, she thought it was probably all gloomily symbolic. The almonds, when left to discolour and age, smelt bitter like arsenic; from sugar to poison, that was how it could be.

Not that Sarah would have categorised her own marriage in that way; or at least mostly not in that way. She understood her marriage to be a compound of what once distinctly felt itself to be love in all its entirety, now bundled with the attrition of the familiar, the predictable, and the deadening of the years since. She saw their relation-ship meshed and wrapped by the sticky ties of children; a weft and weave that frequently availed itself of companionability and good humour, and the ability to share a concern about one of the children with an appropriate balance of maternal and paternal perspectives (mostly, *Come on Sarah, I think you may be over-reacting.*)

Sometimes, she hoped that they were moving towards a state of grace that was mostly founded on gratitude for no disasters shared, and which would allow them to cherish each other in their life together after the children were grown, and would avail them the gift of warm silence and thankfulness. Not that any of this prevented her, occasionally, unexpectedly, looking at the children's orthodontist with an awakening of desire, with a sudden hot longing to be held and kissed by a different man; to slough off her existence as Michael's wife, and be able to place her hand on another man's face and kiss him wholeheartedly. Sarah understood this as an offshoot of the relentlessness of monogamy, but it did not make its occasional emergence any less disconcerting or wistful. Suddenly, in the middle of a street to see a man she found attractive and to understand he was not an adventure that would be hers. (Some women, she knew, did not feel any constraint, but Sarah was a keeper of promises, and would turn her eyes from a quick, connected, gaze. What this told her about herself she felt disinclined to pursue. Introspection, she had been bought up to believe, was a sword that could debilitate as much as clarify.)

As she looked at her face in the mirror and blended in her foundation, calling to the children to get their bags ready for school, and reminding them it was swimming today, Sarah saw that she indisputably looked her age; her skin seemed slightly separate from the flesh beneath, and there was something a little gaunt about her mouth. Each pregnancy, each birthday something slipped softly away until she was somewhere different. Not invisible, but somehow cloaked with a layer of fine dust; her previous, sensual, shimmering young self hidden beneath the sediment of wife, mother and housekeeper.

In the main though, life was good. Michael was a partner in a small solicitors' practice, and specialised in asylum seekers. She had lost count of the dinner parties they had been to where guests recounted tales of people clinging to the underside of the Eurostar train, such was their eagerness to be the recipients of social services and the National Health.

Sarah could only think of the times she had gone to Michael's office and seen men with wary eyes and silent wives, smelling of food cooked in over-crowded kitchens and wearing donated clothes and a crushed, bemused air at where their dignity and humanity had been filed in the process. She was always conscious that for someone who looked into people's eyes for a living, she could rarely bring herself to look into theirs. And so she sat at dinner parties while Michael solidly, predictably, refused to cngagc with other guests' prejudices, and thought of how people's perceptions of a promised land were frequently misplaced, and that her own exist-ence frequently seemed a planet away (was it possible that only last week she had written a letter on behalf of the Council for the Protection of Rural England, supporting their view about a local bridle-way?) and that she was proud of Michael because how to be good troubled her too, and it assuaged her that he so manifoldly was. (*Is worrying about the preservation of the green belt a contribution, or a luxury?* she had asked Michael one night last week in bed, and he had smoothed her hair from her

5

forehead and said *You should worry less about how you fit in*.) In the circumstances, it seemed remarkable that he should be so little troubled himself.

Sarah shooed the children into the car and sent Jack back into the hallway for his swimming kit. She remembered another dinner party where they met an architect who was married to a younger, second wife called Candida. How, Sarah wondered, *could her parents have named her that?* She could not dispel from the woman's cheekbones, from her long limbs and her cropped dark hair, an aura that was bubbling, yeasty, malodorous. And when the architect said, *Unless your first wife or husband is a terrible person, I mean capable of real wrong-doing, I would always recommend staying with them because the alternative is so disruptive and painful for everyone involved*, Sarah watched as Candida's fork stopped halfway to her mouth, as if she might speak then decided not, and Sarah wondered what barrage of chaos lay beneath his words and her silence, and looked across the table at Michael in a small moment of gratitude.

Sarah kissed the children and deposited them in the lane that led to school, and resolved (not for the first time) that she should really think less about what made other people tick. It was not remotely selfless, or altruistic, she understood that; more like doing a jigsaw puzzle, where she was continually intrigued at how others were composed. (At school, a new mother last term who had introduced herself as Cordelia; *Goodness*, Sarah had responded, *isn't that something to live up to? Not at all,* Cordelia had responded, *I love it and I am always the only one.* Sarah had driven all the way to work wondering why she would have considered the name Cordelia such a blow; another expectation to fulfil, when there were so many she felt lay unachieved.)

The architect's comment had sustained her, though, through the period of half a term of school when Michael had been so busy she had hardly seen him, and when she felt like a single parent anyway. When he came home he was terse and irritable with her, and she viewed him as a marginally unfair schoolteacher, whom she could never do anything but disappoint.

She was always intrigued by the point at which these remote standoffs dissolved into more amicable terrain (this time when he had gone into the garden and picked her a handful of purple lilac and wrapped it in a twist of silver foil, and given it to her as she sat at the kitchen table reading the Sunday paper. She had felt awkwardly moved that he had gone outside with scissors, and a length of foil, and done this for her in a way that was unostentatious and thoughtful and made her feel real affection for him as she kissed him thank you.)

Mostly, Sarah told herself, their marriage was good (now, as she sat stationary in the traffic because of the roadworks). If anyone had asked her to describe him, she would have struggled beyond words like conscientious and decent and kind, although she remembered how the curve of his smile, in the early years, had made her stomach jump, and how she had loved to place her hand on the small of his back and feel his spine beneath her palm. Their relationship, she saw clearly, was upholstered by the wadding of their experience shared; each childbirth where he had sat and held her hand, reading her clues from the crossword she liked to do, rubbing her feet with lavender oil and not reacting when she told him, *Oh fuck you, it's fine for you in the spectator seats*. She still knew the things she liked to watch him do; the way he wrapped presents with a neat fold on the cut side of the paper, the way he peeled oranges, and tied knots, the way he could pack suitcases into the car without wasting an inch of space. Balanced against these were the rage she felt for the way he tossed coffee grains into the sink and left them to discolour the enamel, even though she repeatedly asked him to stop; the way he left apple cores in the sidepocket of her car to rot and stink; the way he expected sex as a ritual, a habit, rather than as an extension of warmth of feeling, or as an expression of anything other than his need to ejaculate.

In this way, Sarah understood marriage to be a series of checks and balances, amounting to something that was broadly good, occasionally gratifying, and sometimes only tolerable, but which occasionally made her feel that she had a load strapped to her back which was bending each of her vertebrae until she was so twisted out of shape she could not stand up straight. On these occasions, it was what she felt for their children that made her feel she would always be able to fill her lungs to capacity.

Sarah was aware too that she had spent almost as much of her life with Michael as without him. They had met while at university and married not long after, so the person she could summon up who was not his wife was so young, so unformed, so implacably confident in the face of life, it was hard even to connect with the memory of her.

She remembered riding pillion on a motorbike around an island in Greece, and the wheel catching in a pot-holed road, she and her then boyfriend spilling off onto the verge, her ankle torn and bleeding from the still-spinning back wheel. She had looked at her foot, before the pain had started to bite, before she began picking the small bits of grit that clung to the edges like clams, and wondered how this could possibly have happened. There, in full view of the bowl of turquoise sea, the cicadas singing in the long grass, a frugal lunch of rolls and taramasalata and olives in her rucksack. Sarah realised retrospectively that, aged twenty, one simply did not expect things to turn out badly. Between herself and her friends was somehow an assumption that life was benevolent and they were lucky; so they walked through underpasses late at night and lived in flats in run-down areas, and never for a moment considered that it wouldn't be all right.

She realised, simply, that they were not wired for the possibility of disaster. Was it childbirth, she wondered later, which made women cross a divide between the assumption that everything was benign, to a state of constant reckoning with life; fearful that tragedy and awfulness might lash out at any moment? The loving of something so infinitely vulnerable as a baby, it was that, Sarah had decided, that did for most women. One only had to stand over the cot of a new born infant, hypnotically watching the rise and fall of each breath, afraid to leave the room lest five minutes later the tiny rib cage might not rise – *just at the moment she stepped into the shower* – so that one leaned over the cot making pacts with God or the universe, in order to leave the room and for the draw-in of oxygen to continue.

Most of all, in their early days, Sarah decided that Michael had made her feel safe. She felt she could trust him, that he would always tell her the truth, and that in his personality, what might have evolved as intensity had manifested itself as meticulous attention to detail, and she was comfortable with the knowledge that this exonerated her from the same.

Sarah could make mud pies and decorate them with flowers for the children in the knowledge that the tax disc would never be out of date on the car, and that when they left to go on holiday – perhaps to drive all the way down to Italy – he would have appropriately colour-coded folders with the relevant sections of the map, and before the harmonisation of the euro, each national currency contained in the same folder as the section of the map. (Her mother, Lydia, who had loved a series of emotionally indulgent actors, had said, *God, darling, how can you bear it*, and Sarah had laughed and said, *It's probably the contrast to my childhood that accounts for its appeal*.)

With hindsight she wondered whether that was why her mother had been so unmaternal. Lydia had always been so busy nurturing men who would storm through the door and worry about their art, or, more frequently, the line of their teeth or the timbre of their voice.

Why, Sarah had asked her mother when she was sixteen, *do you always fall for men who make a living pretending to be someone else and being applauded for it? Isn't that, clearly, a recipe for a lack of honesty?*

It's the drama, her mother replied, *I'm addicted to the intensity of it all*.

Even now, in her seventies, Lydia could still be relied on to waft in to see the children, wrapped in an enormous magenta scarf, wearing eyeshadow as green as a pea, and tell them stories of old shows on seaside piers, while they sat and listened, mouths half-open in concentration, and Sarah found she could forgive her all of it because at least she had not aged into monochrome conformity, as she suspected she herself might do.

Michael's mother was so very different from her own, it had been easy to love her too; for her dependability, her kindness, her emotional sanity in contrast to Lydia's. Michael's lack of curiosity

11

about his adoption had always intrigued her. When he told her, it was not announced as some great revelation, as something which might have a bearing on anything at all. Instead he told her as if saying that he had been unable to book a table at a restaurant. She could picture it still, on a picnic by the river, after she had made a joke about hoping their children would not inherit her mother's taste for the fantastic.

The next time Sarah saw Sheila, she wondered who his birth mother might have been, and how she might have been different; at the same time seeing Michael and Sheila together and recognising that her calm hands had somehow infused his. Her own appetite for drama, however, provoked her to ask him: *As a child, weren't you always weaving stories about being a tragically given-up child? Didn't you stand at bus stops and imagine your mother had just gone by in a blue car? No,* he had replied, *as far as I was concerned, as far as I am concerned, I was holding my mother's hand at the bus stop.*

Yet when Sarah gave birth to her first child it was all the more remarkable (she could still summon up Rory, new and bloody in her arms, his mouth a perfect bud, his dark eyes searching beyond him, his fingers clasped around one of hers.) The streaks of her blood, his blood, the white chalky vernix, all of it seemed to reinforce how much each of her children belonged to her: belonged to her in a way that was knotted into her bones, her muscles, her organs, into each breath of hers that had oxygenated them during their nine months in her womb.

When Sheila and Henry came to visit her in the hospital (Sheila smoothing the corners of the sheet and then reaching forward to kiss them both), Sheila took the baby so tenderly in her arms, with such real pleasure in her smile, but Sarah could not stop herself from thinking that her mother-in-law had no genetic connection, no corporeal connection with this baby at all. (Was that part of the process of birthing, she now wondered in retrospect, that one's perspective became so relentlessly physical, biological? At the moment she handed Rory to Sheila it was with the same anxiety as if to a stranger who might not care for him at all.)

When Grace was born and turned yellow with jaundice (her blood tussling with the traces of her mother's blood in her system) it was just another sign, Sarah felt, of how intrinsically physical the knot of motherhood was.

Yet, when she stopped feeling wary of Sheila holding Rory, she felt a small pang of pity (her breasts leaking and throbbing as she sat there) that this moment had never been Sheila's; her birthed, crumpled baby held precious in her arms.

Later, when Rory was about six months old, Sarah looked back on her feelings with a small sense of shame. She watched Sheila feed him pureed vegetable, carefully wiping his chin with the spoon. She watched her sing to him old songs and lullabies, and clap her hands for him, praise him, and cradle him in her competent arms. Sarah pictured it, later, when her children all adored their grandmother, as if Sheila had knitted blood corpuscles and bone tissue out of thin air. In loving them and caring for them, she had biologically meshed them to her.

When Rory's attempt at saying grandma became Fanma (and Grace and Jack followed suit), it seemed so appropriate to Sarah that they had named her for themselves. She felt badly, in retro-spect, about asking Michael whether he had wondered about his birth mother driving past in a blue car. Yet, when she kissed her sleeping children in their beds on a summer night, their warmth on her lips and the scent of their skin inhaled deep into her lungs, she felt again the impact that they were born of her body.

It had all seemed so fixed, so complete, so smooth and steady, until now as Sarah parked the car and began to walk past the supermarket to work with the small hot thought of Harry like a vein throbbing insistent beneath her skin. Harry. First of all, how ridiculous that she should now feel this for Harry. Harry, who had been Michael's best friend since university days; Harry, whose younger face smiled out of their wedding photos. Harry, who suddenly seemed to incite such a longing in her, such a desire to reach out and touch him, that last Sunday when he, Kate and the children came to lunch, Sarah had got up from the table to get something from the larder and had stood with her palms and her forehead against the cool wall and told herself not to look at him, to banish the flush from her cheeks and instead to ask if anybody wanted some cranberry, and check if Jack had been able to cut his meat properly. *Are you OK?* Michael had asked her when she sat down (typical, that he should have noticed her red face.) *Yes,* she had replied, fanning herself with her hand, *I think perhaps I drank the wine too quickly,* aware that she and Harry were employing all their energy not to look at each other, and that their not looking was requiring every ounce of her emotional self.

Ridiculous, also, that this was not some new passion, a new face met in the round of her existence. Once in Spain, she had watched an old olive press operated by a donkey trudging in slow, meticulous circles; with each orbit completed, a resonant creak of the press. It was indulgent, she knew, to see a mctaphor in it, rather than a historical solution to extract oil from an olive, but the tread of her life was familiar and she had not met someone new – at a hockey match while she waited half-frozen for the children, or at the juice bar after yoga, or at the Italian class she attended four sessions of last spring. Instead, it was Harry, Harry in a process that was insidious, velvety, so that even now, as she pushed open the door of the practice and greeted Helena the receptionist, she was aware of a small persistent softness at the base of her throat, and the want of him like a liquid warmth beneath her skin.

Beginnings always made Sarah feel comfortable. She felt that if one could trace things back to their origin, and place a finger right where they started, the ability to do this made eventual understanding possible. But with Harry, how to do this with Harry? Had it been brewing for years, contrary to this feeling of being ambushed, catapulted into somewhere with a landscape that she had not thought to see again in her life. (Again, her mother's voice in her head: *God, Sarah, why are you so indelibly middle-aged?*)

The answer was one she could not expect her mother to understand; her mother who had borne one child before she was twenty and then carried herself as if it had never happened to her body, or her life, at all. Sarah saw herself as a mother first and everything else afterwards, and even though she was confident Michael desired her and that he did not look at her body with critical eyes, she felt it visibly to bear the marks of multiple births. (How did her breasts suddenly become so old, the skin resembling the film of milk on top of a cup of coffee?) As for other men, until now, she had never thought much beyond kissing the orthodontist, and all of her escapist fantasies were most definitely clothed and most definitely fantasy.

But now with Harry, this territory that was so disconcerting, so astonishing. The feeling of standing on ground with a momentum of its own; a torrent of slick, gleaming earth that might slide beneath her feet, taking her somewhere that was very far from the neatness of her life. And in spite of its relentlessness, she knew this neatness mattered to her; a notion of accrued integrity, of time invested in fidelity. On her pillow at night she had told herself, *This must stop*, as if her feelings could be put firmly away like groceries unpacked, and then in her dreams there would be Harry again, and she would wake in the morning with the sense of him dewy on her skin. Easy, too, if she could regard it as an unrequited crush, a small, ridiculous fantasy that would blow itself out like a cloud in a squally sky, but since the day in the meadow, and the prospect of choice he gave her, the choice of how most definitely not to be faithful, she had moved from the olive treadmill to the wet slick of earth, and she could not reach out her hand and find anything to steady herself.

All of it, until the meadow, had been composed of such small moments, such small incidents, she understood that too. A series of deft, slightly awkward nudgings, which seemed to have placed their bodies, their awareness, in this hot-throated place. The first (at least she thought it was; was this the beginning she needed to define?) was two months ago, when through a mix-up they had both turned up early to collect the boys from football. There was a soft rain falling from a grey smudged sky which made them retreat to a café opposite the pitch, the boys continuing to play with their hair plastered to their foreheads. At a table in the window they could just about see the game, and

Harry had leant forward and rubbed a patch through the steamed up pane and she could see Rory, misty-edged, near the goal.

The table had a cloth which was red and chequered, and as they talked (she was laughing at something he had said), she was suddenly aware of her hands on the table, awkwardly rearranging the milk jug and the sugar bowl, in small, self-conscious movements, which reflected, perhaps, that she could not remember the last time she had sat at a table for two with a man who was not Michael. But mostly she was aware of his hands across the table from hers. (Did Kate still see, she thought, how beautiful his hands were; the shape of his fingers, the contours of his knuckles, the white half moons on his nail beds, the blond hair at his wrist?) *Unfair question*, she thought, in the knowledge that she knew Michael was handsome but that she knew this in a way that was objective, long absorbed. It was not something she would have *felt*, felt so that she wanted to reach out and touch him, in the way that Harry's hands, on the red tablecloth, made her feel now. She knew, therefore, she should not judge Kate for not having her breath taken away by Harry's hands on the cloth.

She placed her own hands on her lap, and watched through the steamed up window as the final whistle blew. How could it have escaped her attention that they talked so easily, and with so many similar words to describe things? Sarah was mindful of the fact that she had never known him single. When she met Michael, Harry and Kate were already together. Kate's father had died months earlier, and it was evident, the first time she met them, that Harry had become the central passion of her life. *Harry and Kate*, she had truly never thought of them as anything separate from that; as she looked across the table at a forty-two year old man, and realised that she had always enjoyed his blue, blue eyes. (How odd, how strange, she thought on the way home, half-listening to Rory's account of the football match, suddenly to see somebody as if for the first time; to connote a real affinity that had been there for years.) There, through the years, there had always been Harry, an awareness that all the times the four of them were together, she and Harry had been talking and laughing.

Then, in a small hotel that they had all stayed at recently for a friend's birthday party, Kate had asked to borrow her hairdryer. Sarah went upstairs to their room and knocked on the door. Harry said come in, and told her Kate had just gone down to the beach with the children, and he said *Look at this cherry tree right outside the window* and she walked to the window and looked at the coronet of blossom and Harry stood behind her, but a little along the sill, and she felt very aware of the back of her neck and felt her skin turn warm (impossible that she should be blushing) and was suddenly aware that it would seem the most natural thing in the world to turn and kiss him, all the time the blossom vivid against her eyes. Instead, she said *Yes it is beautiful*, and pressed the hairdryer into his hands (not even trusting herself to look at those, they would be her undoing), left the room, quickly and clumsily, stood at the top of the stairs, her hand on the banister, and told her heart to stop pounding.

Later, on the beach, she watched him throw a frisbee to the boys as Michael lay dozing beside her. She was aware of the arc of the frisbee, the smooth stones beneath her feet, and the salt in the air and it made her breath catch in her throat. Harry turned and smiled at her, and came and sat down beside her on the shingle, and she wondered why she was so acutely aware of each of his limbs in relation to her own.

In the late afternoon, they all walked along a coastal path, and their steps had fallen in beside each other, and he had said something which made her laugh and she was aware of the yellow gorse by her side, and the white, loose, pebbles beneath her feet, and the blue sky and a gull wheeling overhead, laughing with a spontaneity and a sudden sense of liberation that made her feel giddy with the sea air swimming in her lungs. Jack had looked back down the path and said, *Look, Mummy can't stop laughing* and she felt so awash with happiness and so alive and she looked ahead at Michael to anchor herself in the real, in the now, and reached down and picked up a pebble and put it deep into her pocket and clasped

20

her fingers around it and told herself that she must not feel this way.

Momentum, she had decided, was the most dangerous thing. Most things, she was aware, gathered a momentum of their own; good things and bad, small splinters of spite which could crystallise into active dislike, and now this, an awakening of feelings which each day seemed to swell into something more, like a bulb or a shoot sucking in water and light and bursting forth into something huge and juicy and luscious, like an enormous plant which she had to part with her hands to take even a step. Coupled with this was an emergent sensation that it was not her feeling alone. There was something in the way Harry held her gaze, something in the way his eyes sought out hers that made her feel the same transformation was happening within him. Desire, sinuous and thrumming, stringing itself between them.

And then, the meadow. One morning last week, Kate had phoned and said she was unable to get away from school early. Harry had taken the car to be serviced and was stuck at the garage, could she go and fetch him? There was a small blade of treachery, a flicker of guilt in her assent, but undeniably an eagerness to drive to the garage and have an excuse to be alone with him.

When Sarah got to the garage, Harry was standing out on the forecourt, and as Sarah stepped out of the car, she saw him begin to hold out his arms and then drop them to his sides. (It is instinctive, she thought, this feeling that our bodies should behave as lovers' do.) She walked towards him and he said the car was nearly ready, and suggested they drive to a meadow nearby and go for a walk. Sarah said, *Yes, that would be lovely*, the *yes* singeing her lips as she said it, in the knowledge she was stepping onto earth that was gleaming, slick with desire. As Sarah got back in the car she knew that Michael did not deserve this, because he had never doubted her, and yet as she reached for the ignition, she looked at Harry's hand, the length of his fingers, the shape of his knuckles, and it was all she could do not to fold her body over him and take them into her mouth, kiss each finger softly, her hair falling into his lap. So she thought of the children, of what she had put into the boys' packed lunches. She thought of the paraphernalia of work, eye charts, magnifying lens, glaucoma tests, and tried to clutter up her mind with the flotsam and jetsam of each of her days; a trolley with a skewed wheel to push round the supermarket; an authorisation form to sign for a school trip; one of Michael's suits that needed to be taken to the dry cleaners; anything to stop her kissing his wrist.

And now, a week later, she could still not think of any of it with equanimity. Her memory of it pulsed hot and silken, making her want to bite her lip.

Down by the river, the meadow grass long and fluid, the cow parsley stirring, and a cuckoo calling through the lightly leafed aspen trees. A morning

22

in May, the sunlight clear, and the greenness of everything so bold, so surprising, so vivid to the eye after the bleak simplicity of winter, and the ground warm to the touch, and a breeze softly teasing her skin, and the cuckoo's call again through the trees and nobody else there, and she could not bear to look at his mouth, at his hands. The space between them palpable, buzzing, as if their bodies were throwing two magnetic fields and she sat on the edge of a low ruined wall, the stone pressing into her flesh, all the time threading and plaiting a long piece of grass, the green sap staining the creases in her index finger – creases from washing up, peeling carrots, smoothing beds, unloading shopping, marks on her hand from a life so disconnected from that moment, that moment when desire was heavy and palpable in her mouth, when her lips felt bee-stung, her breasts stirring beneath her shirt (still surprising that they should have been summoned so; her body responding to an old call, an old pattern once known) and when more than anything she would liked to turn to him and say hold me, touch me, kiss my mouth.

How odd, how long-forgotten, that the body could dissolve into atoms, each one jangling, vibrant, so unbelievably alive; the heart stomping in the cavern of the chest, the blood into the veins such a flood, such a rush. And all the time, the grass in her hand, her fingers plaiting and weaving and her eyes behind her sunglasses, and for the first time in years, her body, her self, there, as if naked on the grass like a clean-sculpted bone. Besides it the drapes of motherhood, of wifehood; the infinite softenings and kindnesses and steeliness that came from loving children; the complex bundling of the everyday, of working, of shopping, of cooking, of buying birthday presents and school uniform. Instead, it was as if she might have given him her sex in the palm of her hand; held it to him, her body pressed against the wall. Her hands, patient and measured for so many years, tearing at his shirt, at his fly, kissing his neck with infinite tenderness. And all the time, the cuckoo, and the sound of the river, and the skin-warmth of the spring sunshine, and the memory of a novel read long ago, when she was twenty and invincible and wholly selfish, of the river carrying a woman and her cousin's fiancé away, and thinking how easy it would be to surrender to all of this, to yield to this moment, to allow her honey-sticky limbs to do as they would; to think only of herself, of what she wanted to do; to disregard consequences, loyalties, promises long ago made, now, at that moment, on that morning in May.

Harry pushed his hair from his forehead and said, *I can't explain how, how this has happened, but I want you, after all this time I'm consumed by you, I can't think of anything else* and put his head into his hands and Sarah stepped backwards, because more than anything she wanted to step into his arms, but knew that outside of this there were Michael and Kate and six children and that this meadow, this moment, could not contain all the debris and fall-out from all of those lives. So she had placed her finger to his lips so that he could not say anymore; could not sow her longing with words that made it rise up of its own accord, and they got back into her car and drove back to the garage, and the car felt so hot, so unbelievably hot, and Sarah could hardly make her eyes focus on the road before her.

Later that evening, before Michael got home, when the children were playing outside and Sarah was chopping onions for pasta sauce, the phone rang and it was Harry. He said, *I'm sorry, if what I said* . . . his words broken and unfinished and she said *It hasn't* . . . *I wanted to know that.* He did not reply and she said no more, but they stayed on the phone just listening to each other breathe and Sarah was unsure whether her lungs wanted to gasp for air, or not breathe at all; as if the tiniest influx of breath might crack her whole chest. To listen to him breathe – was that a gift that was possible, allowable? – and when she turned back to the onions, she realised she was crying, and recognised that this was what true heartache was: the knowledge of affinity, of passion, curtailed by obligation and duty; the realisation that heartache was not something experienced at sixteen, crying prostrate on the bedroom floor because a boy had ended it all. No, that was not heartache at all. Instead, it was this: her heart throbbing in the expanse of her chest, and all the time patiently, quietly chopping onions, pouring tomatoes from a can and swilling it out for the recycling bin, and answering Grace when she ran in and asked how long supper would be and telling her she could play for another half an hour.

Now, tonight, a week later, the memory of the meadow still tangled in her skin, the drive back to the garage when they hardly spoke but when she wanted to tell Harry all the things she would like to do to him, with him, and the knowledge of how easy it would have been to stop the car and place her hand inside his white shirt, run her other hand through his hair and kiss him softly, climb from the driving seat and straddle his lap and take him inside her. Instead, she had driven him quietly to the garage, her body humming and drenched, her mouth dry with longing. They looked at each other but did not speak as he got out of the car, and at her feet lay the long stem of discarded grass, and she drove back to the house with the windows all down, and wondered how she would ever think of this with peace.

Now, sitting on Jack's bed, holding his hand as he fell asleep, his hair soft on the pillow, his pirate pyjamas blue like the sea, she could hear Grace in her bedroom practising her cello and Rory in his room chanting Latin verbs for his homework, and she thought that these were the sounds that should be anchors, guy ropes; these were the rhythms that both sustained her and tied her to this house. In Harry's house, she knew, the same bedtime rituals would be happening. A flute instead of a cello, pyjamas that were not blue; but Kate would be sitting by a bedside, or checking teeth were clean, and perhaps Harry would be bringing upstairs a glass of water, or loading the dishwasher, or pulling the plug out of the bath. All of it, in both houses, had a sanctity she could see as if it lay on the bed beside her; and she felt at that moment that anything else was inconceivable, impossible. Whatever she felt for Harry could not fracture all of this. Later, Michael would come home and she would grill some fish for supper, and mix salad in a bowl they had bought on holiday in Italy, and they would sit at the table and use the pepper grinder Sheila had bought them years ago and each moment would affirm that this was her life. This was her life, and to jeopardise it should be unthinkable.

Folding the children's towels onto the rail in the bathroom, she told herself it would probably only be a short affair. An affair, perhaps, that would be jewelled with passion and fulfilment, with moments that she could dwell on when she was old and all thought of sex gone. An affair that would consist of sex overspilling from cars, on grass pressed into her spine. Sex, however, that would make her unable to look at Michael or at Kate; sex that would eat hungrily, lustily, into the fabric of all of their lives. An affair that would surely, probably, peter into nothing; a residual embarrassment, a memory of transgression shared and which made all interaction between their families awkward. (A summer barbecue, when they stood on opposite sides of the fire, handing each other a drink, fastidiously careful not to touch at all.)

No, affairs, Sarah knew, seldom ended cleanly or simply, with a civilised, neat step back into the way things were before. She had learnt from her mother, from tirades in rooms below her at night as a child, that love or passion, when it leaves, seldom departs in an even-handed way. And if they were discovered (and now, thinking this, she could scarcely swallow her fish as Michael talked to her about a case he had struggled with today), how bloody that would be, how impossible to extricate themselves from their web of treacheries and betrayals. It could never be fixed; she knew that with the calm resoluteness with which she had gently told Jack this evening that his remote controlled helicopter was truly broken; it had crashed into the fence and would not fly again.

If not an affair, she wondered (passing Michael the salad), what if it could truly be love? A love in the second part of her life which was golden, blooming? A love she had chosen as a woman, not as a girl; for a man whom she would love for himself, not mostly as the father of her children. Then she thought of the architect, of Candida, at a long-ago dinner table. Golden, she knew, would not describe the aftermath. And she thought of a friend who had married again, and who had told her (in a way that was not cynical or bitter, but in a voice that carried with it the truth of knowledge painfully gained) that most times a second marriage meta-morphosed into the first, selfishness re-emerging as the frisson evaporated from watching the new partner sleep. (Now, with a start, she heard Michael say 'You're miles away; what's bothering you?')

And where did that leave her, Sarah thought (now loading the dishwasher, Michael turning on the news, the dog curling up in its basket beside him.) Did that leave her with the knowledge that love could not be sustained; that all love became porous through the tyranny of the everyday, nibbled at the edges until it could not be held up to the light?

Perhaps, she wondered, for some there existed a kindred spirit, a person without whom life would be unlived, but mostly, was the best to be hoped for compatibility, affection; a shared harness worn without chafing or recrimination through the years? Did that mean, then, that she did not believe in the possibility of vibrant love sustained, and if so, how bleak a perception was this of how it could be? And where did that place Harry, when she felt all these things, other than confirm her instinct that she must not become his lover?

In the face of it all, she thought, perhaps the only certain love was what she felt for each of her children; love that was palpable, still thuddingly felt in her chest.

Yet one day, she knew, the children would be grown. Then, they would love her not in the way that they did now, when each day was a web of enmeshed interaction. When they were toddlers she

29

had felt they saw her body as an extension of their own; clambering over her, squirreling into her, pushing their faces into the side of her neck. It had all been – and with Jack still was – so physical, so visceral: the smell of their hair on a warm spring day, the scrubbing of their feet in the bath after a summer day spent barefoot, their small, warm bodies creeping into her bed at night, curling up in the turn of her arm, their heads on her shoulder.

She remembered the days when she used to collect them from nursery, how they would spring into her arms and wrap their legs around her back. She remembered how they used to cry if she left them not yet asleep with a babysitter and coming back from a dinner party and taking Grace, wailing and teething, into her arms. In those days, just holding them was a panacea for most of their woes. They had cried because they simply wanted to be cuddled, or because they had fallen and grazed their knee. The day would come when she would not be able to solve what troubled them; when simply sitting by their beds would not dissolve their anxiety away.

They were growing up so quickly, and soon, she knew, she would not be enough. They would ask to borrow her car keys, and be keen to drive lickety-split away. She would stand across from them in a room, and tell them she understood what they were saying and they would think, dispassionately, *That is not what I meant at all*. They would find her sleeping and think *How did you get to be so old*, and perhaps look at her one day and feel responsibility, not love. *I have become cynical*, she thought, and placed her head in her hands and wept.

The next day, she stood in the kitchen after the children had gone to school. There was a knock at the door and she opened it to find Harry. 'I just had to hear you say no, he said, I just had to look at you and hear you say no'. For a moment, the only thing she could think of was to step forward and say yes, but instead she stood with her palm flat to the door, her gaze somewhere beyond him, to the place where she knew the lie of the land and its relentless exactness, and how it was sustained by commitment and truth. The place where her children and her husband had expectations, assumptions of her; the place where she had deposited each coin of loyalty, of fidelity, over the years; the place where she and Kate stood as friends through years of mutual support; the place where she had stood long ago and made her promise to Michael.

Sarah knew this was not like a random, connected gaze in a street, a flirtatious dalliance that could be forgotten as such. This was a huge shifting of the plates of her life, this renouncing of what was possible, and this snuffing-out of her passionate self. She reached forward and touched his hand, in a gesture that was gentle, remorseful, and said to him, 'We should not, we cannot, I won't,' and stepped back inside the door. And as he walked down the drive, she looked at him with longing and felt her spine stiffen with what she could only think of as honour; honour and duty and obligation and promises long-held, and fidelity and integrity, and a refusal to set herself loose. She thought of it all, and felt it crystallise around her; her marriage, her feelings for Michael, her understanding of what her children needed from her. It clicked into place like a fine lacquered shell, something she would carry for the rest of her days, and she turned to go upstairs and get ready for work.

The phone rang when she was halfway up the stairs. She paused and decided not to leave it to the answering machine. When she picked it up, it was Michael, his voice affectionate and warm.

'Hi sweetheart', he said. 'My case has just collapsed – how about I come and meet you for lunch before you start work? We could go for pad-thai; I think you owe me from when Jack and I beat you and Grace at Cluedo.'

Sarah laughed and said, 'How can you remember a debt so old? From my recollection it wouldn't amount to pad-thai, you'll be lucky if you get a sandwich.'

Michael said, 'I'll see you at 12.30' and put down the phone.

Sarah went upstairs again and stood before her wardrobe and picked out her new jacket, put on her lipstick, combed through her hair with her fingers, gathered up her keys and handbag and went to meet her husband.

Her husband whom she knew she loved and whom she had, quietly, certainly, chosen again.

CHAPTER 2

KATE

To love and to cherish till death us do part

I should assume my husband is happy to see me, Kate thought, and banish this feeling that as he walks through the door it is with a small sinking of his heart. I should assume, she told herself, that it might still be a good part of his day to come home and tell me about his students and college; about some dispute with the bursar, or some change to admissions policy. For our conversation to take place to a backdrop of the children playing or quarrelling or laughing or watching *The Simpsons*, and for the lasagne I have cooked to be a nod to nurturing domesticity and the belief that sitting down for supper as a family laces us more solidly together.

Instead, Kate was fretful, unable to compose herself, her hands unable to lay hold onto anything with conviction. There was a new lack of confidence in her body language – had he noticed that, she wondered, and decided, ruefully, he had not. It had seemed so long since he had looked at her properly. If he had looked properly, it would be evident and clear; this small trickling away of her self-esteem and her certainty, so that recently she thought she might be trailing small, soft grey motes of dust, dust that could be smoothed up onto the pad of her finger and shown to him, saying, *Look, this is what remains of my confidence as your wife.*

In reality, of course (for whatever else she doubted about herself she had always been emotionally lucid, always very clear about what her heart felt) Kate knew what was at the root of both her uncertainty and the insidious self-consciousness which made her feel hollow and pared away. What Kate really wanted to do when her husband walked through the door was to stand in front of him, her arms non-confrontationally at her sides, and say to him, *I think you do not love me anymore*, and as an adjunct of this ask him if he was having an affair.

How well-documented, Kate had thought recently, was the process of falling in love. A list – Kate had always liked lists – could be plucked from the air and would broadly, probably, approximate most people's experience of new love. The visceral tug of an initial gaze across a room; the headiness of a first date; the passion of first sex; the longing to kiss until one could hardly breathe; the glorious drama of a first argument and reconciliation; the tenderness of holding each other soaked in the rain. Frank Sinatra on a CD whilst eating breakfast in bed; a dress worn with no knickers and a light, loose, sway of the hips; Christmas morning and rows of packages beautifully tied with ribbon. No, Kate was very familiar with what Harry, in his social scientist way, would call the iconography of falling in love. It was just the falling out, the desiccation, that wasn't so lucidly documented.

The falling out, she had decided, was composed of small treacheries and cruelties, but even so it had a sinewy, compelling grace of its own. At least if one had the composure, the detachment, to watch it without being burned; like looking at a hotplate and resisting the temptation to press one's hand in the middle. (She was mindful of Harry at the garden centre last weekend, leaning on a trolley while she took too long to decide on a terracotta pot and noticing he was drumming his fingers in a way that was so bored, so detached, that she felt belittled for caring about whether the pot was square or round.)

How hard it was to place these feelings aside; for her heart to remain afloat on her children's love, and to disguise from Harry what she was insightful enough to gauge. And so, as Harry's key turned in the lock, and he called out his greeting, she began to slice tomatoes, the bright seeds spilling onto the chopping board and tried to banish from her mind an image of love distending, distorting; love twisting out of shape before it began to peter away. A bubble of distended paint on a south-facing windowsill; something that would crack open, peel away and leave the wood to rot.

There was no moment Kate could point to and say, *This is when Harry began to love me less*. Instead, it had dawned on her like a tautness, a pulled muscle in her neck; a sensation that something which once moved effortlessly, easily, now required fastidious attention to make it move at all. An awareness of silence, pools of non-words, pools that suddenly now seemed to be congealing, thickening, so that everything said – even a light-hearted observation – seemed to spin and sink below the skin of its surface, her words disappearing from view and floundering in the dark wetness beneath.

There were small moments of frostiness, small signs of impatience; a suggestion – only implicit – that their marriage, once robust like a well-pumped tyre, had begun to hiss air, to soften and bunch into creases, and that Harry was watching the process with an eye that was cool and detached. In bed last week – the day when he had spent hours waiting at the garage and Sarah had fetched him because Kate had been delayed at school – he had lain in bed and sighed, a huge heartfelt sigh which she had taken to communicate that he was both weary of her, and all that they represented.

It would be possible, Kate thought, if one had enough *sang-froid*, to write a list of all the things one's lover used to do; all the things that marked one as chosen, as loved, replaced with the gestures and actions that confirmed one was not.

French kissing, her list would start with that. The moment at which the intimacy of mouths filled with each other's tongues was replaced by the chasteness of a kiss on the forehead, as one might kiss a recalcitrant godchild whom you rather would not. For weeks now, when Harry left for college, he had smoothed away her hair and kissed her on the forehead. How sterile it felt, how dry and unyielding, when physical intimacy gave way to the perfunctory, the obligatory.

When they were out together – perhaps for dinner with friends, or even going to a parents' evening at school – on no occasion did his hands touch any part of her body at all. She wasn't looking for gestures that spoke of intimacy – like holding her hand, or lightly touching her hip as she walked first through a doorway but instead, tiny gestures: helping her on with her coat, passing her the salt and his fingers overlapping with hers. Instead there was this separateness, a notion of having completely vanished from his radar so that her body span, untouched, in a galaxy of its own.

Earlier in the day, Kate had sat in the staff room and marked books, eating the houmous and red pepper roll Harry had made for her that morning, but which, as it sat plumply on the unwrapped foil, seemed to express a duty of care, rather than a manifestation of love. (Now, reproving herself, how could a packed lunch tell her anything at all?) As she peeled her satsuma, she considered whether she was partly responsible for whatever had happened, wondering ruefully how she was meant to teach twenty-seven eight-year-olds, raise her own three children, remember to send birthday cards and still have the resources, elasticity and energy to be fascinating to Harry.

Having children had changed her, Kate recognised that. Before Oliver was born, Harry had been at the centre of her every thought. Later, she felt she could barely turn her head from her babies at all. Some of her friends had felt saddled with the physicality of it all, but Kate had embraced it wholeheartedly, and cherished its physical interdependency. She had not minded the sticky fingers clasping her skin, her hair, the small patches of saliva on the right shoulder of all her clothes and her coat. Watching them, loving them, had compensated for all of that; their small, determined hands clasping bricks, puzzles and beads; their attempts to sit up becoming straight-backed and perfect, their shuffling crawls turning into wobbling steps and then fleetness of foot.

In those years when she had stopped teaching and the axis of her world had become the perimeters of the house, it had been glorious and all-consuming; a time when she felt each day to be a revelation, although she did not know whether she would have confessed this aloud either now or then. Sinking exhausted into bed at the end of the day, it had been with a tiredness that felt wholesome, honest and complete and which evaporated by the morning and restored her ready to do it all again.

Even now, when Oliver was ten, Emma eight, and Drew six, Kate still felt it to be the role which gave her life meaning and morality. She knew she would always regret the absence of a baby in her arms, still, sometimes in the supermarket, look at a baby snuggled in a car seat and want to press a repeat button and have her children babies once more.

And in all of it Harry had been constant, supportive. In those early years, she was struck by how effective they were. He was always comfortable about helping with the children; there was never that division of labour which would have made her feel stereotyped, marginalised. They had, all things considered, a contemporary relationship, and when Drew started school and Kate returned to teaching, it was just as likely to be Harry who made their packed lunches in the morning, just as likely to be Harry who tested them on their spellings homework. Her mother had once said to her, *It's so very different from in my day* and Kate had wondered if her observation held an implicit criticism; of her father, of Harry, of either of their marriages, she could not tell. She waited for her mother to elaborate but she had not, and Kate knew that she would not speak further.

Her mother had always been reticent about speaking about her father. After his death, Kate had waited for moments of outpouring and recollection. She had primed herself to be sensitive to how her mother might react – whether she might suddenly sit down in the chair in the kitchen, press her hands to her face and say, *I didn't expect to miss him this much*, or whether she might refuse to change anything about the house so that it was exactly as he had lived in it, the memory of his presence undisturbed and clear. Kate expected to find her sitting, weeping in his study, perhaps with his books in her lap, seeking consolation there.

Six months after his death, when none of this had happened, Kate wondered whether in fact her suppositions had been about her own grief, not her mother's, and that perhaps she lacked the insight and perception as to how it might have been for her mother at all. How, then, she wondered, do you mourn someone with whom you have spent most of your adult life? For her own part, she regretted not sitting in her father's study more, as autumn had decayed into winter and the leaves plastered against the window sill, before her mother tidied the room up, efficiently parcelling it into bundles, keeping some things and disposing of others. (The surprise, in a cupboard, two years after he died, to find all of his shoes, still beautifully polished, the laces tied with care. Had her mother sat alone in the kitchen one night, the shoe polish tins at her feet in a spectrum of colours, and carefully polished them all, each shoe held firm by the heel of her hand, and then placed them in this cupboard and never said a word?)

There was always a clarity about her mother and objects; a composure in her efficiency which was particularly striking at that time. So, although she waited for her mother to spill memories like match-sticks, to pick through recollections of her married life and share them with her, it did not happen (instead, Isobel talked of learning to play bridge, speak Spanish) and Kate wondered if it was all too personal, too private, to share with her.

As a child, Kate remembered sitting in the back seat of the car, her parents talking to each other, their voices masked by the hum of the engine, and herself surrounded with so much space and a half-formed, half-understood notion of exclusion, of adult interaction that did not include her and to which she had no alternative. Her own decision to have three children was tied to a residual memory that as an only child, she was both central and peripheral to her parents' marriage.

Tonight, driving the children home from after-school care, as she refereed a spat of elbowing, kicking and jostling for territory and Jaffa Cakes, each child convinced of their blamelessness (*He started it!* ringing through the car), it seemed unreal that her own car journeys could have been so placid and peaceful.

When her children squabbled and fought and said dreadful things to each other – yesterday Oliver pulling out a clump of Emma's hair in a fight over the television – she was both appalled and secretly glad, for she felt somehow this asserted their own rules of engagement, and that they would be stronger, somehow more equipped to deal with what life threw at them, because they had honed their toughness on each other.

Kate wondered if at any point memories ossified and became constant. Was memory ever final or finished? Did it ever sit, complete, or was it constantly, subtly, being appraised and re-evaluated and understood in a way that depended on how it stood in the sequence of one's life? Would she ever think of her marriage, her parents' marriage, and say, *It was this* and understand it to be so. Her own marriage, which had been one thing, now seemed to be something else entirely. Was it only death – in its final, complete, full-stopped way – that made memory conclusive?

Her father had been dead for years. Could she hold her parents' relationship up to the light and understand clearly, finally, how it was for them? And in doing so, in seeking to understand theirs, could she learn anything that might help her to re-align her own?

As a child, Kate had seen only clarity, simplicity in her parents' marriage; a balance of contrasts which perhaps was the key to why it had worked. (How ironic that would be, when her own generation had fought so hard to level the ground, to equalise the roles and blur the differences, if hindsight revealed it did no good at all, that delineation had been the key to it all.)

The problem, she saw, as Harry began to ask her about her day, and they laid the table together and he opened a bottle of wine, was that there was no hook of discord to hang this all on. Kate tried to remember the last time they had really argued, and could not recall any significant division. It occurred to her that she had rarely, if ever, seen her parents argue, and certainly not the plate-smashing, retina-detaching eruptions that some of her friends described.

In her parents' marriage, Kate was never really aware of anger, or arguments. Instead, there was a feeling of equilibrium, like the smooth, easy trot of a horse. A calmness and peace that came, she suspected, from knowing what each other was for, and having expectations accordingly. They had always been different, so very different, and to her child's eye, and even now, their differences created a balance and a symmetry which made sense to her still. Now, as she carried the lasagne to the table and reached over to Harry and kissed him, aware of a small sinking despondency and a dip of her heart as he did not return the gesture, absorbed in his own thoughts. She put knives and forks on the table, pulled a serving spoon from the drawer, and wondered if it was so much to ask to be kissed on the lips.

She thought again of her father – in truth she could not remember how he had greeted her mother when he came back from the surgery. She remembered, though, how he had greeted her, and how the whole beat of the house lifted when he walked through the door. Her father had been the energetic heart of it all. Her memories of him were always mobile, laughing; scooping her up in his enthusiasm, challenging her, teaching her; encouraging her to take joy in whatever lay in reach. She remembered him lifting the head of a hellebore from a frost-studded ground in January and saying, *Look, look how perfectly beautiful this is*. Her father had been like a trade wind, carrying with him spices, pistachios and rosewater from hinterlands, from places that were always new, and laying them in her lap like shiny buttons or jewels. Whether it was teaching her to play chess (the *fianchetto* with relish; the *Sicilian* on a day in November when the rain lashed at the windowpane) or how to recognise a Norman spire on a church, or how to paint with watercolours to capture the quality of light, or how to listen to a piece of music and understand its composition, he had always talked to her, always shared with her, and she could still summon up how that had made her feel. It had been so easy, as a child, to know that she loved him. It was simple to locate; vibrant, responsive, and tangible, there, in the middle of her chest.

With her mother everything had been quieter, more understated, a calm remoteness which Kate had not wholly understood for years. It was not, she had always known, that there was not warmth or love. Her mother loved her just as much as her father, but preferred things to be contained, more composed. There was peacefulness in that – and she had recognised this more in her adult life – recollecting sitting with her mother and learning to knit and to sew, or listening to her mother read to her, her voice so careful and precise in its expression.

Her parents had been as two magnetic poles in her life, allowing her to walk a path somewhere in the middle. And now, as she struggled with the small, palpable rejection of Harry's unreturned, unnoticed kiss, she remembered a trip to the beach when she was about twelve: her father absorbed in a rock pool, explaining to her the hierarchies of the creatures within, and then standing by his side as they skimmed stones into the water, the pebbles bouncing three or four times as they flew out into the bay. And as they did this, her mother moved amongst the sand dunes, picking samphire and laying it in a wicker trug, her head wrapped in a headscarf, a moss-green cashmere cardigan tied around her shoulders, stooping and standing in a way that was sure-footed and secure. Kate had looked up towards her and felt respect for all the things she knew how to do, for her dignity in the way that she did them, and for a curious bravery in the way she moved amongst the dunes, alone. Now, she had never felt more alone or so uncertain as to how to behave. I have no template for this, she thought, as she began to spoon food onto plates.

That her parents' relationship had been happy Kate had never doubted; there had never been anything to suggest it was anything other than harmonious and good. It had been so clear-cut, this was what struck Kate now; what Robert had

45

expected of Isobel and what she had expected of him. He would return from work to find her perhaps in the garden, pruning a rose or staking a clump of lupins, and there would always be something perfectly-judged cooked for supper; a tart made with neatly arranged concentric half-moons of apple. Her mother would play the piano while Robert read in his favourite chair, and the dogs would lie on the rug and the clock would chime in the hallway, and Kate would feel as if she were living in a story book, where the world could be counted on to be affluent, and smoothly even, and safe, and measured out in accountable beats of goodness, with a rhythm that was recognisable through the seasons and through the years. Often, at Christmas times and birthdays, when she had stood in shops wondering what to buy as a gift for Harry – a painting, an i-pod, a beautiful trout rod that he might never really use – she was reminded of how her parents' gifts to each other were always appropriately chosen; a fig tree, a chess manual, a watering can of pleasing proportion, a piano made of walnut, a book of essays on ethics. She saw in this an easy understanding, an intuition about who they were that allowed this to be so. She recollected her mother being given a rose and saying (with more emotion than she usually expressed), *It is perfect, it is exactly what I would have chosen*, and remembered thinking that she wanted a husband who bought her birthday presents which made her feel that.

Kate called her children to supper, and thought perhaps she should try to talk to her mother. Perhaps she should go and visit her and say, as if holding out something broken in her hands before her, *Look, this is my marriage, what shall I do?*

At the table she looked at each of her children; at Oliver trying to separate out the red pepper from the lasagne to avoid having to eat it; at Emma grating some Parmesan in a neat soft drizzle; at Drew holding his glass to Harry and asking for more water, and she thought that the five of them were sitting around the table in the kitchen, eating food she had prepared and talking about their day, and that perhaps this should be enough. Perhaps I am unreasonable to still want more, or to yearn for something which perhaps must pass with time.

But it was not just that (now, as Kate scraped the leftovers from the plates into the bin, and told Oliver repeatedly to help load the dishwasher); it was the sense of there being someone else, someone beyond their supper table of five, which made her feel that she could not ignore it at all. Perhaps it was a student; a young, glossy-haired, long-limbed, perfectly toned undergraduate, for whom Harry represented an adventure, some kind of rosette. (She knew it was always the beautiful girls who slept with the dons, as somehow an affirmation that they were both beautiful and clever, that their perfect peachiness could entrance minds more accustomed to academic complexity; a small, vivid proof that nothing was as captivating as an arched, supple spine and the smooth, dewy skin of the young.) Or, perhaps it was one of his colleagues, someone fearsomely bright and focused; someone who could discuss his latest paper, rather than mark school SATs exams; someone who would leave small volumes of poetry in his pigeonhole rather than text him to ask him to collect the dry cleaning. Someone, she worried, as the essence of that someone hovered over her kitchen and smoked between the crockery in her hands, someone who was somehow more tempting, more fascinating, even though she wanted to remind him that she had been all of those things once.

'I need to go to my mother's,' she said abruptly to him (Harry was washing the lasagne dish, she could not fault his fairness.) 'She phoned earlier and I said I'd go over once you were home.'

How easily a lie springs, spontaneous and fully-formed from the lips, Kate thought. Perhaps this was how it had been for Harry, two nights ago when he called to say he had been delayed, perhaps a lie rolling smoothly and confidently down the phone line to catch in the curl of Kate's ear. Perhaps a woman, a girl-woman, beside him as he lied to her, putting the phone down and holding her face as he kissed her.

How would it be, she wondered, if a marriage became based on, and sustained by, lies, great chasms of not telling, great boulders of untruth; until finally, one day, it allowed only a vision of the world through the cracks in between.

Suddenly, more than anything, she saw that she needed to go and see her mother: whether just to stand in her hallway and hear the familiar clock chime and feel that all would be well, that this fracture was something small and containable; or whether in seeing her mother, and in being re-assured by her competence, she might feel more resourceful in the face of something that might not be contained or made small.

Kate wanted to watch her mother in her unchanged kitchen, watch her make things that resonated back to her childhood. Hollandaise sauce, pale and creamy, in a blue-striped earthenware bowl, a Victoria sandwich filled with raspberries that tumbled ruby-red from the sides, *coq au vin* with the shallots brown and gleaming. She wanted, ridiculously, nostalgically, to be making fairy cakes and placing crystallised violets in small puddles of icing. To feel enrobed in her mother's composure – that would be a good place to begin.

'Can I come?' asked Emma.

'No', Kate replied, 'you need to do your flute practice. You'll see Granny tomorrow when she collects you from school.'

When Kate arrived at her mother's house, she pulled into the driveway and sat for a while. Through the open window, she could hear her mother playing the piano, a taut, complex melody that seemed to weave through the trees. To her left, in the paddock, stood the old chicken ark. Her mother had stopped keeping chickens not long after her father had died. The ark was mildewed and weather bleached, and surrounded by fescue grass, and the whole paddock was awash with vetch and Michaelmas daisies. There was a softness and a fluidity which eased her eye with the watching, and she recalled an old rooster who used to strut the length of the post and rail fencing. She remembered collecting eggs with her mother in a straw basket with a pink and green stripe, and a Cotswold Legbar that used to lay eggs that were the palest blue. Before Easter, Isobel would save them in the pantry, and they would be there in a bowl on the breakfast table when Kate woke on Easter morning. She recalled, with a smile, all the breeds her father used to collect; an Araguna with feathers that were violet in sunlight; a small Buff Pekin bantam with plumes of feathers at its feet, and silver laced Wyandottes that looked like hand-painted doilies.

Was it all so perfectly crafted, or only how she remembered it; the mind eager to shape memory into small, clear, suckable tablets? All those moments, all those singular moments of beauty (there was nothing to compare with a pale blue egg still warm in the palm of one's hand), combined to evoke a childhood that felt so secure, so aesthetically rich, and which was still so tangible it was as if she could take an in-breath and be submerged by it again.

Kate looked at the house, at her mother's herbaceous borders, and the long stems of the roses which were arching up around the window. The shadows had grown long on the west side of the driveway, and she was aware of her mother coming out of the door towards her, her hands extended in greeting, one of the dogs down by her feet.

'This is a surprise,' she said, 'I hadn't expected to see you.'

'I had a staff meeting,' Kate lied. 'It finished early and I thought I would surprise you.' (Two lies in one night, she reflected, from someone who habitually told the truth, feeling her falsehoods lodge like small stones beneath her ribs.) She followed her mother into the house and breathed in its familiar scent – a combination of flowers (always on the hall table), and wallpaper, and leather armchairs, and thick blankets folded on the side of the couch, and, tonight, a faint smell of elderflower (her mother was saying she had been making and bottling cordial in the day.) It all seemed so solid, so grown-up, and reassuring and she was struck that not only did she still require its solace, but that she was not providing this kind of touchstone for her children, for how could the chaos that was their home evoke any of this?

How easy it was to doubt everything once self-doubt started, she reminded herself. Her children were happy and loved, and this was not about that. (And anyway, she reminded herself, in the end, how much power could all of this have? All the beautiful handmade bedspreads in the world could not stop one's husband from dying, or loving someone else.)

51

Instantly, she could summon up the memory of her father's funeral: the hearse leaving from the house, on a dank, drizzly day in October, a pallid sun low in the sky, and the rain spitting on the black polished car, and her mother beside her looking somehow both frail and strong, her gaze steady and her bearing upright, when it was all Kate could do not to lie on the gravel and sob, and thinking as she got into the car that it all felt impossible, it could not be happening, her father could not have left all of this when it was so clearly stamped with him.

'Would you like some tea?' her mother asked her. 'Or perhaps some cordial, I think perhaps I may have made it too sweet. It's for the fete in a fortnight, I need to write labels for the bottles.'

Kate said she would like tea, and went and sat in the chair by the grate stacked with kindling. She looked at her mother's sheet music, open on the piano, and thought, as she had often done, how self-sufficient it all looked; knowing later in the week Isobel would sit at the kitchen table and write out labels for the cordial, her handwriting balanced and neat, her fountain pen looping china blue ink.

In the kitchen she could hear her mother pulling the kettle across onto the Aga, a sound transferable back through the years. Its familiarity, its soothingness, made her eyes unexpectedly mist with tears and she focused on the wall, at a small sketch her father had done while at medical school, of a frog dissected on a clean white tile.

It blurred through her tears and came into focus again, and it struck her how neat and fastidious, how careful it was. Somehow, it was at odds with all her father's mercurial energy, this calm, clear diagram of a frog and its innards. And yet, when she had asked him about it and why he had kept it all these years, when so much of what he drew or painted was full of colour and life, he had told her it was because it reminded him how to look, how to really see, that if one did not look properly, carefully, one did not actually see at all, and that seeing clearly, that was the thing to aim for. And now she would have liked to ask him, *What if seeing hurts?* in the knowledge that he would probably have told her it was important to look all the same. And Kate added the frog on its small white tile to her list of the process of becoming unloved, deciding that a dissected frog, with its innards systematically picked out, was probably a metaphor for how it actually was.

'I'll put these by your bag now so you don't forget them,' her mother said as she reappeared with cake, two jars of chutney and a bunch of asparagus. 'The asparagus is beautiful this year, and I made the chutney with carrot and ginger and chilli. There's also some cake which the children might like.'

Isobel sat down, and Kate was conscious of a small pause in which nothing was said, but there was something in her mother's face which suggested she was puzzled by Kate's arrival but would not ask further. So, whilst Kate knew that what she wanted to say was, *I need you to help me, to tell me how to fix this. I think Harry is having an affair, and the prospect of him not loving me is breaking my heart.* Instead, she heard herself ask something about asparagus beds, and confirm that both Oliver and Drew loved gingerbread made with pecans and raisins, and half-listened while her mother told her about a W.I. talk about reintroducing red kites into the hills in Oxfordshire, and Kate could hear both their voices, their conversation, as if it took place in another room, and wondered why she could not, so absolutely not, say what her heart felt.

She thought of her wedding day, a year after her father's death, and being dressed in her bedroom upstairs by the seamstress who had made a sheath of ivory satin, seemingly invisibly stitched. Her mother had stood by the mirror and told her that she looked beautiful, *like a snowdrop*, she said, and she reached out for her hand and kissed her in a moment of real intimacy. A little later, in the church, Kate had stood in the doorway, and prepared herself to walk down the aisle alone (no-one, she had told her mother, could replace her father in that, and she preferred to walk with the memory of him by her side than to arrange to be accompanied by someone else). The church was filled with flowers that her mother had arranged, and the air was crammed with the scent of roses and lilies and jasmine, and as she walked down the aisle her eyes met her mother's before they met Harry's. Her mother's bearing, her uprightness, her pale blue suit, seemed to express a belief that all would be well, that marriage was sustaining, and that Kate could expect it to be as fruitful for her. Kate had looked at Harry at the altar, his eyes smiling, his face beautiful to her, and she saw him through their courtship; on a beach with fine sand pressed to his skin; on a walk through a wood in November when the ground rang clear with their tread; in a turquoise pool, when his body sliced though the water beside hers; at a bus-stop in the rain, when he held her to him, his hair wet to her cheek. In all of it she saw that she loved him truly, and she spoke her promises to the vicar with her voice ringing happy and clear. And now, it was as if she had no voice at all, sitting in her mother's drawing room, her hands folded in her lap, her insecurity like a chill frosting on her skin.

Isobel was asking about collecting the children from school, and who had after-school club (Kate wondered if perhaps she was repeating the question, had she not been listening at all?) and she answered her and then stood up, as if preparing to go.

'I ought to go, it's getting late,' she said to her mother. 'Drew needs his hair washing and there are nits in his class at the moment so I should probably go through it with a comb.'

For a moment, she hesitated, her tongue touching her teeth as she considered a rush of words, then asked instead what music her mother had been playing when she arrived.

'Chopin,' Isobel replied, 'I seem to have returned to Chopin. When I was young I always thought it was tortuous, ghastly, and now I am captivated. I've been playing this piece each day and I think I am almost there.'

'Don't let me interrupt you any longer,' Kate said. 'I might sit in the car and listen for a while. It sounded so beautiful when I arrived.'

She kissed her mother's cheek and left Isobel standing in the room, her hands clasped together in front of her, looking, questioningly, at her daughter's face. And Kate looked at her mother's hands, hands that gardened, pruned plants with knowledge and confidence, played Schubert and Chopin, cooked *clafoutis* and *osso buco*, and gathered elderflowers from hedgerows, and were old, and weathered, and long-fingered, and short-nailed. She looked at her own hands and felt they were weaker, softer, less competent and capable, and that somehow to have had hands like her mother's would have been some kind of help, have some kind of usefulness in whatever she should be doing.

Kate walked from the room and out of the hallway into the drive. She saw her mother resume her seat at the piano, the Chopin beginning to weave its way back through the pear trees, and she stood by her car with her index finger tracing her lips and wondered why it was that she could not share what she felt. Did saying it make it unavoidably real and true? She sat in the car and listened while her mother played Chopin in a room

56

of gathering shadows, and avoided weeping by summoning up the rooster on the post and rail fence.

Kate drove from her mother's house to a lane down by a mill stream, and sat on the old low bridge and watched the darkness fall. The cow parsley by the bridge moved softly in the night air, and under the willow there were tangles of May flies and gnats. She heard a bird calling from the other side of the river, and a cow lowing across the greenness of the meadow. Had she not told Isobel because she did not want her to worry; did not want to trouble her mother's implacable calm with something she could not solve or fix? Was it a transition between who was the child; between who protected whom, and who knew most? Perhaps not, she thought wistfully, recollecting that before leaving her mother's house, she had wanted so badly to run to her old bedroom and lie for a moment on her girlhood single bed, with its bedspread of blue, tweed hearts and mother of pearl buttons and close her eyes and imagine it all perfect again, and Isobel downstairs playing a piano scale that was flawless in its evenness.

Perhaps, rather, her silence was somehow more dismissive. Maybe her mother had no wisdom to offer; no experience of an unhappy marriage with which to enlighten her. No notion of anything other than loving, smooth, easy interaction. Perhaps, she considered, happiness cannot comprehend unhappiness at all. Perhaps if asked, her mother would have opened her palms to the ceiling, and said, perplexed, *Your father and I were happy, I don't think I can guide you in this.*

So the answer was not there, with her mother, in her mother's house, and her father could not help her, and she did not know which way to turn. Perhaps to Sarah, or maybe to Jane, a friend at school? And there in the darkness she realised she could not talk about it at all; that the first thing this had taught her was that the matters of her heart were private, and that there was something so deeply humiliating in all of it, she could not phone up Sarah and say, *I think Harry does not love me anymore.*

Kate got back into the car and began to drive home. When she pulled into the driveway, she turned off the ignition and opened the door. The May night was still warm, and the darkness hung in soft thick folds. Drew's bike lay discarded to the right of the porch, and Emma's stilts were propped up against the drainpipe. She could see a skateboard, a trowel, an old watering can, and all of it seemed like the entrails of her family, caught in the moonlight, waiting for the morning to make it animate again. There was always a sacredness in the sight of all their abandoned things, a pathos she could not shrug off because it signalled so clearly their absence. She could smell the wisteria that scrambled up around the south side of the house, and the honeysuckle that she had planted with Drew when he was only a toddler. The air was thick with their fragrance and she stood still on the gravel and breathed it deep into her lungs. It smelt of summer, of goodness to come, and she wanted, suddenly, desperately, to believe in the possibility, the hopefulness, of it all.

Kate turned the key in the door and stepped into the hall. The lights were all off, and she gauged that Harry was already asleep. She took her mobile from her bag and checked that there were no messages. She had been gone for hours, yet he had not thought to call and check she was OK. Such casual cruelty, such lightly-judged thoughtlessness – another item on the list – capable of slicing right to her heart.

Recently, on a train to London with the children to see an exhibition at half-term, a woman on her right had received a flurry of texts. One – she could not avoid seeing – had said, simply, *i want u now* and she imagined how that might feel, sitting on a train bound for Paddington, to know that your absence had summoned desire and longing, not simply a wish to know what time you might be returning. What would Harry text her she wondered, with a small, wistful, smile. Perhaps *i don't want u now*, or more dishearteningly, *i don't want u at all*.

She stepped quietly upstairs (when had her tread become so silent, so sure footed?) Perhaps through the years of walking with babies not quite asleep, completing circuits of the house dressed in pyjamas and old hockey socks, knowing, beneath the carpet, the line of the warm pipes that ran to the boiler, and able to tread the length of them like a gymnast on a barre, avoiding the place in the hallway where a draught blew through the crack in the door, and all the time patting and stroking her babies' backs, waiting for the moment when their breathing was steady enough to put them back in the cot.

As she stood on the landing, Kate heard one of the children murmur in their sleep, and felt, as she always did when the only one awake, somehow the custodian of all their wellbeing. Awake while they slept, it was as if she could string their breaths like beads on a wire, gather them in her hands and keep them all safe. Often, at night, she strained her ears in the dark for the approach of any harm; got up from her bed, pulled their covers into place, picked a teddy up from the floor, closed a window when a storm rumbled across the hills. And always the sense, in the silence of the night, that she ought to be on guard. On guard against what she could not really say; just somehow wary of what the next day might unleash, about how life might suddenly splinter across her children's chests. And Kate understood, suddenly, clearly, as she dimmed the landing light, that the question that should pre-occupy her was not what it was she had, but, rather, what she *hadn't*. She thought of Harry kissing her years ago on a beach in Morocco and the feeling that whilst her heart swooped and danced and all her senses rang, something quietly, calmly, deep in her bones, told her she would always love him. Now, as she picked up a towel from the landing carpet and saw that she had expected it to be always the same for him, and that the prospect of losing him was beyond consolation.

Kate went first to Oliver's room and sat on the side of his bed, smoothed his hair from his forehead and kissed him as he slept. His face was changing, it was more evident in repose, and she could see the small changes to his jawline which told her that his face would not look like a young boy's for long. It was all there, just beneath the skin, his teenage self ready to emerge; even now, his feet were already a size bigger than hers. She looked at his room, at his fort, at his Lego Mindstorms, and gave thanks that he had always been such an easy child; her first-born with whom she had served her apprenticeship.

On Emma's bed, Kate folded away a game her daughter had been playing, and picked up a pony-tail band that would otherwise be searched for tomorrow. She made sure Emma's teddy was snug in bed beside her, and kissed her daughter and hoped that she would always be loved.

What she would tell her of love, she did not dare to hazard. At that moment, it felt audacious to even presume to tell how it might be. She wished that her children would never feel the accrued sediment of rejection. She would tell them, when the time came, that there could be extraordinary love, and to hope that it fell in their laps, because

61

she could see no other mechanism by which to infer how it bloomed.

At Drew's bedside, she simply scooped him into her arms; he had kicked off the covers, and his skin was damp with the warmth of the night, and she knew he was so deeply asleep he wouldn't be disturbed. How could it be that only one of her children was small enough to do this; that only one of them remained so little as to be folded and wrapped in her arms? She breathed in the smell of his hair, and the residue of toothpaste around his mouth, and momentarily wanted him never to be too big to wear dinosaur pyjamas. She rocked him close to her and then tucked him back into bed, checked that his window was closed and that he wasn't in a draught, then resisted the temptation to fall on her knees and give thanks for them all.

Kate walked into her bedroom where Harry was lying asleep, his face turned away from her side of the bed, his arm across his temple. She went into the bathroom and slowly undressed, and listened to the stillness outside, and the cry of a pheasant in the field beyond. She looked at her body and felt overwhelmed by the things she should do; floss her teeth, exfoliate, moisturise, put a pumice stone to her heels; *how*, she thought ruefully, *did just maintaining it all become such a task?* She decided to skip it all, and to simply brush her teeth, sweeping her hair up into a clip and splashing her face clean.

Kate got into bed, and pushed her feet down into the depths of the duvet. Harry turned, so that he lay on his back beside her. From the depths of her memory, she recalled a poem learnt long ago at school, about a visit to a church and the tomb of a Lord and Lady. The poet had noticed a stone dog, carved at their feet, and that the couple held each other's stone hand. She wondered how she and Harry appeared, lying so still, side by side; their bodies aligned but not touching, intimate and familiar yet without connection. Under the duvet, she edged her hand across the sheet, and found his hand, softly curled, by his hip.

Kate reached out and took it, and felt his fingers clasp hers, and thought, as she lay there, how easily satisfied and comforted we can be. How a small gesture can be construed as some kind of symbol, some kind of allegiance, some affirmation of a long-ago loyalty. A manifestation of shared endeavour, sustained through years. Ambushed by tiredness and beginning to spin down into sleep, Kate knew that even the smallest thing can be construed as a symbol of hope; lying there, holding her husband's hand in the dark, listening to him breathe and wondering how many breaths they had shared together in sleep.

CHAPTER 3

ISOBEL

Discreetly, advisedly, soberly

Tonight, as I sat and Looked at my daughter as she stood by the door, there was something in her stance that was so reminiscent of my own that it was all I could do not to cross the room and change it; brush away from her features a look that carries her origins right back to me. There was something in her eyes, something not said, that was it mostly, but also a feeling that part of her had been filleted, a water of bone sliced from her shoulder-blade, so that as she stood by the door she reminded me of a wounded bird, nursing a small dark bruise that she would not share with me.

I was close to asking her, to saying, *Whatever is wrong?* but felt constrained by the knowledge that she may find that intrusive. I have never been candid with her, never spoken truly openly, despite considering that we have a relationship that is almost all for the good. I am conscious of the irony in all of this too. Her father has been dead for almost twenty years, yet I am confident of the fact that were he to walk through the door, she could, within a moment, tell him the truth of her heart. It was always easy for them to speak in this way; there was always an openness, an ability to look each other right in the eye. I did not feel excluded by this, or in any way resentful. I think one must accept that some people have more spontaneous congruence of thought. With Kate, despite my intentions, I think I do not make it easy. In truth, I think I do not make it easy for anyone at all. There is about me a reserve, a frosting I cannot shed, something cold at the edges that baffles exchange.

This isn't to say that our relationship is not good. Compared with many mothers and daughters I think we stand on mostly solid ground. She has never stood and hurled hot, angry words at me; never blamed me for things in her life that were traceable to me. I have tried, to the best of my ability, to support her in all that she does; to be loving and kind, and to help her whenever I can. More so, in the years since her father died; the knowledge, never explicitly stated between us, that he was the centre of her life, that it was him she could turn to, always him who could provide just what she needed.

It strikes me how much the world has changed and moved on since Robert's death. It is almost inconceivable that he lived his life in a world that was without mobiles, without e-mail, without websites; without tentacles of communication that make accessibility an assumption. I feel as if somehow the world has speeded up. What used to take days can now take moments; a holiday booked on a computer, an aeroplane ticket bought, a grocery delivery ordered, a crossword clue sourced and answered easily. It makes Robert belong, in my mind, to a world that is suddenly old-fashioned, cocooned. A world that somehow allowed more privacy, I think this is what I mean.

In other ways, I find it hard to accept that so much has changed (impossible, really, to conceive that I might get a text message confirming the altered meeting time for bridge), whilst things that I planted in the garden just before his death continue to bloom and grow in their own unchanged, forthright way. A rambling rose that has scrambled almost to the top of an apple tree; a forsythia that is a blaze of colour across the west wall of the garden in spring; a wisteria that is so laden with flowers as to perfume the kitchen through June. So much that he would recognise, so much that he would know, and yet a keynote that is more insistent, relentless, and which I see in so many aspects of Kate's life.

It was easier, I think, for my generation when we married. An over-riding assumption that we might have a little job beforehand, and relinquish it soon after. Not for all women, I acknowledge that; even then there were the fiercely bright ones, striding forth as G.P.s, as university lecturers, as scientific researchers with confident hands and strong voices who somehow combined jobs, multiple children and a knowledge of Elizabeth David. But for most of us, it was softer. An assumption of aprons worn for housework; an ability to polish fenders or arrange flowers depending on background and money. A climate of waiting for one's children to come home from school; of being unable to drive cars; of asking one's husband for housekeeping. All of that is what has been well and truly vanquished, although I can see it has brought other complexities in its turn.

Kate's experience of being a wife and mother is so different from mine. I see the juggling scramble she has between the children, her job and the house. I see how it chafes against any time she might have with Harry. I see how the two of them seem constantly to manoeuvre to maintain it all. Sometimes they remind me of the child with his finger in the leaking dam, plugging in holes, dashing from one part to another. In some ways, I can see that the whole thing is more balanced, more sharing. I never lost the faint element of surprise when Harry would sweep off one of the babies to change a nappy, or to put them in the bath, or when he would arrive though the door with a carload of grocery shopping. Yet I also see, sometimes, how it seems to be built on thin ice; a careering haphazardness that seems somehow to be centreless, with no adhesive at all.

I wonder how it will be when my granddaughter

is a woman; what she will choose, and how it will be for them. For I can see, in retrospect, how it was for women of my age, constantly pictured in our 1950s aprons, looking thrilled holding Hoovers or standing by new washing machines. Whilst powerless in the commercial sense of the world, I think we were anchors and guy-ropes, working like gravitational force to make everything rooted and stable, facilitating what was around us to bloom. Were we as powerless, I wonder, as successive generations would have us believe? Now, when I read of children with little or no experience of mothering at all; when babies of a month old are lined up in cots in daycare centres, their feeding times entered mechanically on a chart?

All this has been the minefield through which Kate has had to walk, and I have supported her decisions, even on the occasions when they would not have been my own.

Yet today, as she stood by the door I was so sure she would say something, something that would spill out on the carpet like a bright red stain. A pause that I filled in by offering to collect the children from school; a new scramble for words while she clarified who had football practice, who needed to be reminded to bring home their flute. A diversion which allowed her silence to trickle away, allowed her to say to me that she must be going, she hadn't meant to interrupt me at the piano. A moment which allowed her to kiss my cheek and leave, allowed me to turn back to the piano and

68

continue the Chopin that I had been playing when she arrived.

Through the bay window I saw her pause and listen to my playing, her hand to her lips for a moment, and then a small straightening and stiffening of her spine. What was contained in that gesture I cannot bear to think. Cowardice again, that I did not run and say, *Tell me what is it that you feel?* Old habits dying hard; my tendency to see but not say.

And now that she has gone, I can clarify my anxiety. As she stood there, there was something familiar, something that carried me back to before Robert's death; as if she were about to repeat all my mistakes. Not mistakes from now, from this part of my life. My widowhood, I have to confess, sits freely upon me, like a comfortable, soft shoe. It was wifehood that taxed me, I can confess this now.

My life now is full of things I find easy to do. I have learnt to play bridge, I have taken a GCSE in Spanish. I go on art-study tours to places like Siena, and become part of a group of like-minded people, listening with absorbed interest to a historian while he explains the detail of a fresco. And afterwards, I will sit in a restaurant and eat pasta and drink wine, and talk with a reserve that discourages any confidences shared. People at arm's length, I find, are easier to deal with than close-up. I am reluctant to listen to another woman's whispered exchanges; a pale lipped,

69

hotly-working mouth, describing a bereavement that has left her at sea. Even less do I want to hear the heartsores of an elderly man; still bereft in a home whose intricacies and workings remain unfathomable. I am comfortable with what I believe is called closure on all of that.

At home, I am still active in the village community. Last September, I held a class to raise funds for the church, teaching some of the younger women in the village how to pickle and preserve. We made jams and chutneys all day in my kitchen, until there were rows of jars, amber on the windowsill, and the house was filled with the fragrance of peaches, blackberries and ginger.

I am part of the rota for doing the church flowers. At Easter time I cut masses of greenery from my garden and make the altar look bursting with spring, the dark green contrasting with the white and gold of the surplices and the cross. I am on the village fête committee, and write gently persuasive letters in the newsletter, asking for bric-a-brac, or cakes for the tea stall.

And always my garden, there was always my garden. My hands are able to grow things with a freedom that I never had with emotions. Each summer brings cascades of colour and fragrance, my trug filled with flowers, the house in its turn. I think I am most at peace on my knees in my garden, my hands pushed deep into the soil, my fingers sure and strong. I have a confidence with flowers, in my ability to juxtapose vibrant colours and scent, to intersperse textures and shapes to create borders that are bold. All this I have never had with people, with emotions; instead a coolness best suited to the making of a good Victoria sponge, finding harmony and peace in ingredients properly weighed and measured.

I like order, and decorum, diligently imposed. I like to be in control, and for nothing to be blood-red, raw. My hands are perfect for making good shortcrust pastry; handling dough with calm certainty, crimping edges with mathematical precision and neatness. When Kate was a child, I taught her to make small iced cakes; willing myself not to correct her when she did not place the decoration in the absolute middle.

And in all this, I can see an amplification of how I behaved as a wife. My home was a plethora of things in the absence of the animate, with me at the centre of a calmly accessorised life. Perhaps I was too fastidious, too tasteful for my own good. I finally understood, in the years before Robert's death, that one could orchestrate context, but not orchestrate love. And it was a knowledge of this that I think I saw on my daughter's face, like a small shard of glass, impossible to extract.

I met Robert when he was just finishing at medical school. I had been at secretarial college, and had started work for a local solicitor. I took shorthand, typed letters, supervised petty cash; sat at a desk dressed in a neat twin set and tweed skirt, asking people to take a seat in reception, and ushering them through when Mr Macdonald indicated to so do.

It is interesting to me how I thought of that stage in my life. I never considered it would be more than a stopgap, a brief interlude before my real life began. I met Robert at a lunch party given by a friend. I noticed him instantly, how his energy seemed different from the other men there. My experience of men was limited to the sons of my parents' friends, who came to the house for tennis parties in the summer, and who all had the same manner, the same bearing, the same correct pronunciation. My mother had always made it implicitly clear; I would be expected to make a match that was decent and sound. The consonance of the heart might have been one thing, but the affinity and compatibility of background another, and I was aware from the outset that Robert would only just qualify.

There was something about him that was less polished at the edges, something about his enthusiasm that was more naked, more raw. Something about the way he answered, when spoken to, that showed he had little time for the veiled nothingnesses of polite conversation. Something I understood later as a lust for life, that marked him out from the other men there. A hunger, I can see now, that I identified but did not share, and did not understand for many years hence. Instead, he had attributes I was able to file under *dashing*, and I considered his inquisitiveness, his energy, a foil for my own composure.

I wonder still what he thought of me that day. I look back on my friends and myself and how we appeared, how we looked; neat and cool in summer dresses and kitten heels; matching gloves even though the day was warm. We weren't debutantes – it was not as polished as that; but we were affluent middle class young women, lined up in a pastel row.

The first time he spoke to me I was standing by the herbaceous border, looking at a rose intertwined with a clematis. I have forgotten what it was about it that attracted my eye. In those days I had not shown any interest in gardening, I had simply sat by my mother's roses reading a book, or walked in her knot garden enjoying the architecture of the box, and taken it wholly for granted that it should be so. It was only a number of years later that I realised how much it took to bring it all to life. But then, I suppose, it must have been indicative of an interest that would later emerge, the fact that I had broken away from my friends, and was absorbed in the garden. When he came and stood beside me, I was aware how close he stood, how he looked me straight in the eye when he asked me what I was looking at.

I was aware of blushing, but that would have been as expected, and I remember not really saying, not being able to say. I remember him bending down and pulling up a small weed from the root of the plant, brushing the soil from his hands with a gesture that was decisive, clear.

He felt strong and bold, standing next to me in the afternoon sunshine, and he felt like someone who would not be intimidated by life.

Always this fear, one I have never really outgrown, that most times, life pecks away the edges of oneself; diminishing and making you less the person you began. Life a small beak, hard and persistent, to be resisted only by order and ritual. Robert, I felt, would somehow not succumb to all that; would somehow resist being cowed because of the way that he was. As he stood next to me, I could sense no trace of fear; instead there was a hunger, a reaching out beyond himself. I sensed he was brave in a way that I was not, and it was this that attracted me to him, I understand that clearly now.

I remember taking him to meet my parents for the first time, and going for a picnic down by my uncle's lake. I sat and watched while he talked to my father; learnt effortlessly, quickly, how to tie flies for trout. His hands were supple and dextrous, the flies lined up in a row beside him. My father smiling, it all being just as he hoped.

In retrospect, I wonder what it was that he saw in me; perhaps someone as yet unformed, a well-bred girl whom he would somehow fan into more life. Perhaps he thought he would wake in me a responsive vitality, basing his opinion on that first day in the garden. I did not mislead him, I am confident about that, but I think I could attribute to that first encounter the suggestion of a sensibility on my part that was not what it seemed.

Perhaps I am wrong, and what he saw, and wanted in me was a balancing calm; that I would be composed at the centre of his world. Flowers on the table when he returned home at night. Or, perhaps he misinterpreted my competence and mistakenly saw strength. Confused aptitude for substance when they are separate things.

Whatever it was, it provoked his proposal. In those days, everything was so much quicker than now, fired on, I think, by the confines of chastity; my insistence that any deviation from a chaste kiss on the lips was not what nice girls did. When I said yes, my parents were delighted; their assumptions, my expectations, duly answered. It was, I can see, like a stitch falling neatly into place; a sampler that would describe with unbroken continuity the trajectory of my life. My mother took me aside before the wedding to discuss the business of the bedroom. Nothing, absolutely nothing, prepared me for the invasiveness of that.

After we had been married about six months, and filled our first home with some pieces of furniture from my family; after I had sewn curtains for each of the rooms and established with the butcher which cuts of meat I preferred; after I had resigned my job to do a few secretarial hours at Robert's practice, re-ordering prescriptions, arranging for home-visits for the frail; after all that I sensed some kind of hiatus, a sensation sometimes that his gaze lingered upon me, as if waiting, perplexed for some kind of answer, for some kind of response to his emotional Morse code. If not my own coda, just some sort of echo, a sign of some eager, spontaneous grabbing at life. Instead, I think he began to see me as a silent pool, where his words, his energies, his love, fell traceless to the bottom.

My keynote did not change, I can see that now. It remained consistent, as it was at the start. There was no hasty scrambling to life like a small apricot tree in spring with the promise of sweet fruit through long summer days. Perhaps he had thought I was like a sapling, a thin slip of willow; supple, elastic, ready to stretch to the light. He did not anticipate, rather, that saplings turn into branches, and branches to trunks, stiff and unyielding. I could not shake off a perception, as he lay beside me in bed, that all was not as he had hoped, as it seemed it might have been, for him.

There came, eventually, the realisation that what appeared to be the uncertainty of my youth had in fact effaced disinclination. A reticence I could not overcome when it came to matters of the flesh. My cheek turned away, unable to look him in the eye; aware of him above me, searching my face. His tongue in my mouth making me want to lace my lips closed and press my face to the pillow.

When I became pregnant I knew from the first movements, flutterings and jostlings deep down in my abdomen, that I would do this only once, this invasion and abandonment of my inner self. The feel of elbows, of insistent feet, pressing and pushing away at my ribs. A photograph I have of

76

myself then, in dogstooth trousers and a smock; my face turned away from the camera, my belly huge.

When Kate was born, I thought her beautiful, yet was appalled at the milk which leaked from my vein-streaked breasts. My nipples glistening, beaded with white; Kate's mouth like a pink, round clamp. I asked Robert to organise some bottles and formula, knowing that I would feel more comfortable with a bottle in my hand, and Kate contained in the turn of my arm. I asked him to bind my breasts; to strap them to me to help stop the milk. And when he sat on the side of the bed, and wound and wound the crêpe bandage, I felt relieved that my innards were again sealed away, I welcomed my old self, wrapped cool and tight. Robert assumed his bedside manner, doing as I asked but failing to hide the disappointment in his eyes. As if somehow I had failed in something he had hoped for, or that in this request, something wider was confirmed.

Yet astonishingly, there were never any molten words between us; no room reeking of acrid accusations or blame; no Robert, white faced in the kitchen, raging that it was not as he wanted it to be. Instead it was amiable, kind, and always polite. Friends came for supper around the oak table; me lifting and spooning something glorious from a dish, Robert at the other end of the table carving meat, pouring wine. In the midst of what was not right, I always loved the exactitude with which he carved meat. And yet, I caught occasionally, as he turned half-away, a flicker of something – was it sadness? – in his eye. In bed, when he reached over to embrace me, my response was at best dutiful, measured. What excruciating words. After a while, he ceased to try at all, pained by the fact that it had so little effect or that I closed my eyes at the first instant and so obviously wished it done and over.

So we became as parallel lines, united in shared purpose, with Kate resonating in between. When she was tiny, I dressed her always in white so that she looked like a small snowdrop, perfect and clean. I know now, and I knew then, that I was not an instinctive mother; irritated, despite myself, by her small sticky fingers, by her knocking over a drinking cup, or fidgeting on my lap when I read her a story. I was frustrated by her emptying out my kitchen cupboards, by the splashing of water over the side of the bath. But all of this did not mean that I loved her less; instead, I knew I would enjoy her more as she grew older, when, as a young girl, she would become more measured and moderate. Robert, meanwhile, adored her from the first instant, her body snuggled close to him like a tiny rabbit. There were always silvery saliva trails on his shoulder, her small fists, insistent, tugging at his hair. Out in the garden, he pushed her on a swing from the cherry tree, her cheeks wild and red, her mouth open in laughter, her scarf untied and flailing in the wind, one glove visible on the ground by the terrace. Robert read Greek myths to her, and taught her to play chess, her hand swooping down to the board when she captured his queen. And I would look forward to the times when he was not there, when she would sit quietly beside me and I would teach her French knitting, when her body would be quieter, stiller, more in tune with mine.

As I sit here thinking all this, I am aware of new patterns, new symmetries. I can see myself as I was when I married him, as I was when I buried him, and count the grace notes of the years in between. The moments when our marriage changed from one note to another; a small, hidden pulse, altering the key. A solidifying of assumptions, of habits, an implicit drawing of lines; a nod to separateness, to a life lived amicably but without engagement. I did not doubt his fidelity, he was too much at home for that; mostly in his study, which I hardly ever entered. On the occasions that I did, I found it brimming with his things; books piled high on the floor, tubes of oil paint, chess games half-played, one of the dogs always flaked out in front of the grate. I was perturbed by its disorder, its riotous mess, by his serial absorption in one thing after another. And I continued my steady, metronomed life, once objecting to a friend of Kate's, considering her to be too challenging, too confrontational, and Robert said I should see benefit in that. I wondered then, if that was what he had concluded; that what I valued most was the mediocre, the tame, the subdued. The aesthetically pleasing at the expense of spirit. A veil of order, of composure, that subverted the life within. The irony that I understand that better now, now, when it's too late to change, if change were ever an option.

So instead, I can hold everything that happened up to the light. I can see Robert, and Martha and myself as we were at that time, like paper folded into a complex shape, different from each angle, obscured in part. I can remember the time – we had been married almost thirty years – when slowly, fraction by fraction, I noticed a change. A feeling that all his restless beating and tapping had suddenly found its focus. A fervour in his eyes, an urgency that took him away from the house. A perception that his gaze had moved entirely elsewhere, carrying something before him, as if a glass orb in his hands. Sleeping beside me, yet rapt in his dreams.

There are always signs, anyone whose husband has had an affair will tell you that; there are always moments when something does not quite fall into place; a tiny lie; inexplicable lateness, a spring in the step when one is only opening a gas bill.

Then, in the church with Madeleine Sawyer, both of us working on decorating the font; some complex attempt at softening austere edges for a christening, so florist's wire in one hand, sponge in the other, and buckets of ivy and cream lisianthus at our feet. Madeleine began to describe how she had bumped into Robert recently (*Well, not exactly bumped into*, she clarified, *perhaps he hadn't seen me, these encounters happen so quickly. Back in the car before one can be sure.*) A small, resonant crowing detectable in the tone of her voice.

'With a woman,' she continued, 'with a woman in Dorchester churchyard. Perhaps a friend of the family? A cousin of sorts? But no resemblance, quite different really. Looking at a stained glass window, clutching books like tourists. Perhaps in a little club, some sort of interest group?'

I asked her to describe her, feigning a need to be reminded of whom she might be, and Madeleine's voice gathered pace, nibbling and nudging at but avoiding the word common. She left it hanging like a trapeze between us; my husband and his common mistress gleefully spotted before a stained glass window. All the time that she spoke I continued to loop flowers into the green, compact sponge; a dislike of cream lisianthus that has persisted to this day.

When I got home, I thought of something Mrs Bolton my housekeeper had said, talking of her brother-in-law and waxing the splashback as she spoke. *You don't have to scratch very deep*, she said, *most times when there's a change there's usually a woman involved.* And I knew this was what Robert was carrying before him; his feelings for this woman staining his hands like saffron, detectable even to my detached eye.

81

Later, when he was not yet home, I sat ice-still in my favourite chair, and wondered how to interpret it all. I felt as if I had a lapful of tiny mosaic tiles that needed to be re-grouped into an image that was different from before. Old loyalties, trust, I could see all that had changed, but what surprised me most was that I felt no real wound. No laceration, no stinging sense of betrayal; instead a calmness that belied what I thought I should feel. When he came home, I feigned sleep in bed, and watched him through my lashes as he undressed and washed. My husband, my unfaithful husband, was this how I was supposed to perceive him now?

It was easy to find her number in his telephone book; easy to call it and listen to a man I presumed to be her husband asking me if it was about ironing and to call back later when she would be there. My first shock was that she was some kind of washerwoman and I remembered him reading Beatrix Potter to Kate as a child, and saw again Mrs Tiggywinkle with her starched apron and ample girth. And I knew, in the centre of myself, nuthard, resolved, that what I wanted was to see her, to make the picture whole. I was bothered less by his transgression than by my partial view. What this tells me about myself I have still to learn.

I took eight shirts of Robert's to her on a morning in June, and stood on her front step while she battled to open the front door. I realised my mistake; in houses like those I think the front door is not often used, but I stood my ground and let her struggle with the bolt. I sustained myself with the thought that I knew who I was about to see, whilst she did not; that I could look at my husband's mistress and hand her his anonymous shirts. When the door finally opened I was struck by her stockiness. A plain, busty woman, sucking the knuckle of her right hand. Her hands were like Mrs Bolton's, that's what struck me first; her hands so familiar, her nails cut straight across. I saw a small blood blister pooling at the base of her index finger, those hands that must have held him and touched him in a way that mine did not. I balked at their plainness, at their strong-fleshed knuckles, and wondered at their capacity for tenderness, for care. Yet as I stood there, I felt completely composed, resolute, my mouth bone-dry; the emeralds of my ring winking as I passed her the bag of laundry. She was common, Madeleine Sawyer was right about that; one of those decent, working class women most easily described as that.

In the car afterwards, I sat gazing at nothing, the key in the ignition but incapable of driving away. Humiliation? Bemusement? Something of that. A splinter of surprise that this was what he had chosen. In my mind, she assumed an air of Mrs Tiggywinkle, a smell of moist earth that I associate with her still. But most of all, a small palpable shock, that I had expected the extraordinary and was confronted by such ordinariness. I thought that love should make exceptional marks, or should stand out like a four leaf clover, different in shape.

But perhaps, I conceded, it was another failing of mine, that I simply could not imagine what he saw in her, simply could not imagine what they found to talk about. Simply could not comprehend how she was beautiful to him.

That night at dinner, sitting almost in the half-light, a candle on the table softly hissing and flickering, I knew that I sat there armed with the truth. Yet I did not question him, did not confront, did not ask him to justify, as he sat at the other end of the table and asked me about my day. I wondered what he would do if I said I had seen Martha, had stood on her front step and given her his shirts. Would he have dropped the bowl of potatoes he was holding, I wondered, thinking, despite myself, of how much that would distress me.

I sat and calmly cut my Dover sole, eased and lifted the bone from the flesh. I looked out beyond him, through the window to the skyline, at a small bat flitting across the lawn. Was it cowardice, I wonder, that made me sit there like that; not asking, or confronting, or telling him it must stop. The memory of Madeleine Sawyer's words looping and lacing the edge of the font. Humiliation, surely, was what I should feel, and embarrassment, betrayal, in the face of his infidelity?

And yet for reasons that I could not explain, as I sat there quietly peeling an orange, the rind curling, slowly, onto the plate; slicing the pith cleanly from the flesh – the reassuring feel of the dessert knife in my palm – I realised suddenly (as the bat swept by the cherry tree, as one of the dogs began to bark in the hall) that what I had always liked, had preferred, was the clarity of objects, calm in my hands. Things, objects, that were easy to orchestrate, to collate, not like people with their mess, with all their entrails. Robert's study, brimming with his restless mind. His body that had obviously wanted love. I watched him, sitting there, taking grapes from the bowl and not using the scissors.

For I realised that night it was not love re-directed, not love re-channelled from me to her. Rather that what he felt for us could easily be set side by side. His kindness, his politeness, his respect for me, juxtaposed with that passion, that rawness, his love for her. I sat at my dressing table, unpinning my hair and brushing it smooth, hearing him showering and then cleaning his teeth and wondered if he had washed from his skin the stickiness of her. I looked at his body, at his almost old body; unbelievable somehow that it should be stirred so. How close it came to ridiculous, the whole thing always ridiculous anyway. Sex, in my mind something like a seed dibber, poking away, making holes inside.

I watched as he came into the bedroom and buttoned up his pyjamas, his feet pinked from the hot water, as I took grips from my hair, hearing them plink into my porcelain bowl. I thought suddenly that he looked tired, yet expectant, as if he thought I might have something to say. I wrapped myself in an armour of non-words, asked him what time he would be leaving in the morning, told him Kate was staying the night at a friend's.

Then, as I lay beside him, aware that he slept, I listened to the rise and fall of his breathing. The man to whom I was married who did not love me; realising what we thought in our beginnings was love was perhaps never it at all. The knowledge, nascent in the bed, that I was perhaps more comfortable with its absence.

In the night, when I woke with pins and needles in my arm, I sat up and shook it and bent it, flapped it like a fish on a deck, and Robert woke up and asked me what was wrong, and I said, *Nothing*, so he rolled over and back to sleep. And before that night, I would have told him, would have asked him to massage my arm, but now, resolutely, doing it myself. My fingers kneading the flesh above my elbow, the junction of my bone and the string of my vein. Where my blood flowed no business of his. One small punishment in the face of it all.

In the morning I stood on the landing before a portrait he had painted of me. I am dressed in blue, before a stone hearth, my hair in a chignon, my hands in my lap, my back perfectly straight, my mouth composed. I remembered, when I first saw it, how I was struck by its austerity, and wondered if that was what he saw, this rigidity of my bones. The painting whispered that it had not been enough, that I had not been enough; as if his eye was drawn to the window and beyond. Perhaps, even to the possibility of her, like a bowl of fat cherries, just out of reach. Perhaps, even while he painted it, to the reality of her; whilst I sat austere and cool like a fire screen between.

Otherwise, apart from that night, the next two years unfolded unchanged. A small awkwardness on my part at the acknowledging of birthdays and anniversaries. I bought him a shirt for Christmas and imagined her unbuttoning it. A birthday card in which I felt unable to write *with love*; instead choosing a benignly humorous one that allowed me to sign my name with a quip. A reticence on my part, when receiving birthday gifts; one year, a rose bush, so aptly chosen by him and beautiful next to the fig tree. Conscious, despite everything, of how well he knew me. And so accepted with gratitude, with a smile of genuine gratitude, for occasionally it can be no-one's fault that things are not as they seem. Our wedding anniversaries were probably the most awkward; once Kate cooked us a meal and I could hardly swallow a bite. The notion that our marriage was like an old weather-beaten flag, beleaguered on a sandbank, with no connexion to any life at all. And when Kate proposed a toast and said *To thirty-three years*, it was the only occasion I remember when he did not meet my eye.

So all of this continued until a morning in October, when I saw Henry Malpass running up the drive. His face looked flushed and urgent, he was still wearing his stethoscope. I remember it swinging wildly and wondered why he wore no jacket. I thought it odd on a morning like it was, to be in his shirt sleeves with the mist hardly lifted. He came into the kitchen and asked me to sit down, and I was aware of Mrs Bolton, in the hallway, switching off the Hoover. He told me Robert had died of a heart attack in the surgery, and I sat there stunned, taking his autumn-chilled words in. He made some tea and an awkward attempt at holding my hand on the table, until I lifted it away and placed both my hands to my face. My first thought was for Kate, and how this would devastate her; for despite what had happened between us he had always remained rustling and crackling at the centre of her life. I was aware, in truth, that he had left me long before, that in fact his death had made my separateness more honest, had slaked the tissue of pretence from our final years.

It was therefore with calmness, with resoluteness, that I could comfort Kate, that I could go to the undertaker's and see him there in his coffin, the undertaker walking softly at my side. The awkward reverence of this business of the dead, with satin-lined coffins and eyes respectfully averted. I sat and looked at him, smooth-faced and finally still, and talked with Kate of what he liked to do; remembered trout flies tied by a summer lake, and how he had swung her in his arms when she was a little girl. I talked of how he pushed her on the swing in the dappled shade; how he had once gone to seven shops to buy the perfect shade of red bike. And all the time I looked at him, my hands clasped in my lap, I was caught between wanting to shake him or to stroke his face; to punish and tell him that he was a fool and a cheat, and that what he thought was kind was indeed not. Or, to tell him, at last, that I understood, and that much of the blame was mine.

I thought, in spite of myself, of Martha, and how she might be feeling now. Whether, in fact, she knew, or was waiting for him at an assignation not kept. I thought of her on her doorstep on that day in June, like an old-fashioned ship in the full sail of his love. I wondered how she would learn of his death, and thought she would give anything to sit where I sat now. My words to him were compromised, nibbled at, frayed at the edges. Hers, I felt, warmly holding their truth.

And as I looked at him lying there, smooth and distant, somehow everything became suddenly clearer to me. In death, it was as in our married life. When stripped of aesthetics – flowers on the hall table, strawberries picked from the garden, *boeuf en daube* for supper – this was as it had been for years. I saw that I had preferred to be separate; that love with its hot sticky messiness was not to my taste, its erasing of where one person stopped and another began. I wondered, not for the first time, if that knowledge had pained him.

So it was at the funeral, surrounded by waves

of sympathy, washing over me like sickness and making me press my lips with my hand. Yet I wept softly in the pew; for his life lost, for his love lost, for his love for her; for all that it had taught me about myself. I wept for the end of my married life, its uniformity, its order, its predictability. The control of superficial uncertainties, that was what I cried for most.

At home, afterwards, all those people, all that consoling. The taste of lies, of pretence, like cobwebs on my face. Wet oyster mouths telling me what a good man he had been, my arm patted and stroked like a child awake in the night. Serena Malpass saying how fine he was, and I looked right past her, through the window and out to the herb garden, saw the parsley tangled in the rain, and wanted desperately to eat mouthfuls and mouthfuls of parsley, anything to ease the surfeit of cloying words. To say, with a polite pause, that he had not loved me for years, but that he had behaved decently and kindly and that in the circumstances I could not ask for more. Instead, I nodded, and chewed the edge of my lip, averted my eyes, my mouth full of the taste of falsehood. I looked at Kate on the other side of the room, pale and sad, struggling to accept that his death had happened at all. I was mindful that one day she would have all this to learn, this business of marriage, this surrendering of self.

Later in the afternoon, when everyone had left, when I had refused well-intentioned offers of help with the stacked china and lipstick-lipped glasses, I went for a walk, when the house was quiet and the shadows of dusk gathering. I decided to walk to the churchyard, to the graveside, to strip away the memory of the morning's murmured excesses. I wanted to stand beside him and be alone together; to acknowledge the realisation that there was still a tie. If not love, knowledge, knowledge of how it really was, and beyond that the familiarity of what we had shared. I stood in the twilight, my hands balled deep in my pockets, the air cool on my cheek, and thought that what bound us now was artifice, perception, and her. And then, I saw a book I recognised pushed into the soil, pushed into the wet soil of the burial mound and knew instantly that it had to be hers. I understood that she had come here already and stood with him too. Martha, who had unwifed me.

The knowledge, in truth, that I had unwifed myself. Strapped myself in with routines, rituals, accessories; long-ago breasts wound tight in crêpe. So this was what she had offered to him; a wreath of visited churches her homage to him. I resisted the temptation to hurl it into the hedgerow, and decide to take it home and put it with his things. A perverse satisfaction in completing the circle.

And when the business of mourning was over, when I had stood before his wardrobe and sorted his things; heaped shirts and jackets into bags for Oxfam, suddenly, surprisingly, being unable to part with his shoes. The sound of them, on the path, through the walkways in the garden, always the sound that signalled he was home. But otherwise, when our bedroom was purged and empty, I asked Mrs Bolton to make up the bed in the red room, telling her our bedroom was too big for one. Two weeks after Robert died, I slept in a single bed, the sheet ironed and tucked tight, the blanket heavy. I felt so perfectly, so neatly self-contained. I felt so clean – thinking of the French word *propre* – feeling so *propre* in my own neat bed. Lying in the dark, a false girlhood upon me, my failings, my awareness, heavy on my chest.

I asked myself what it was that I had ever felt strongly about. Wondered if the word passion could ever have rung true from my mouth; and felt, sinkingly, dryly, knowingly, not. Lying there, feeling my desiccated innards, my old walnut womb, pickled in loss.

I accept that this is how I have lived my life, accumulating accomplishments and accessories in the absence of feeling. I have never seen, in my sleep, a mouth above me. I have never stretched forward to lick the outline of a lip. I have never stirred at the line and shape of a man's neck, never wanted to kiss where it flows to the shoulder. I have never looked at a man naked and asleep, the skin below the navel soft and pale, the hair dark and curled, the flesh scooping away. Never wanted to place my head there and wake him with my mouth. The salt taste of a groin. Was that how it could be?

When Robert had been dead a month, I decided to tidy his study, to sort things for Kate to keep and to throw some away. In truth, it bothered me, it was like a room interrupted; its chaos, its business, belied the fact that Robert would not come back. His desk looked like the desk of a man who had just stepped out to make tea, to stroll once round the garden, or to sign at the door for a parcel.

Most of the things were easy to order; books that I put alphabetically on shelves; a dusty old insect collection that I gave to a neighbour's child. Almost squeezed-out tubes of paint that I threw in the bin; a pair of his slippers that I gave to the dogs.

I found a diary of sorts that I had been unaware that he kept; a brown leather volume filled with years of things that had caught his eye. A page that recorded appropriate clematis pruning, whether to cut to the ground or just to the joint. A sketch of a brown-tailed moth spotted on the blackberry hedge; white and thick-winged, unusual this far north. An observation, one year, that the viburnum had been glorious, noting that the flowers were at least four inches across. A sketch of a spire, the crocketing beautifully done. A record of a chess game, had with himself. A verse from a sampler scribbled down. A daub of paint in a blue that he said caught the sky that day. A sketch of an egg, the shell painstakingly etched. An outline of a Chinese honeysuckle flower. Some lines from a poem, heard on the radio. And then Martha, Martha on a day in May.

A saddleback roof. An extraordinary woman. Catching sight of her as I looked up from my book. As if suspended in the quietest, calmest, most luminous moment of my life. And later, *the feeling that my life had not really started until now. All that it is began with her.* Pages and pages of where they went, what they did. A tumbling, a grabbing, a seizing at life. I had not understood that their relationship was so animated, alive; ours, in comparison, like smoke through my fingers.

The last entry was written a few months before he died. *M. Always M. For this I give thanks.* Then the entries dwindling, his mind and his heart on her. His restlessness ceasing, his world complete. In reading the diary, I could see it all. The workings of the heart, frequently too expediently placated, for them ringing clear through the baggage of their lives.

In a cupboard by the desk, I found the rolled-up canvases. The paintings he had done, and which finally completed my understanding. We were a series of portraits, Martha and I, my portrait the first picture, Hestia, the goddess of the hearth. One small storage jar behind me on the mantelpiece. A window behind me, where his eye looked beyond my calm blueness to the garden beyond. My territory the solidity of the hearth, the sanctity of the home and all of it dissolving in the face of the other. And Martha, I understood her to be Aphrodite, the Goddess of love and laughter and sex.

Her first portrait was called 'Aphrodite Ironing',

and she stood in a small garden ironing shirts. Her body was broad and fleshful and strong, her arm poised at an angle sweeping up a shirt sleeve with the iron. Her legs looked like they were rooted in the soil, as if in a second picture she might become a tree. There were butterflies around her, but not naturalistic butterflies, instead painted so thickly as to look almost enamelled, jewel-like. Wings of topaz and turquoise and amber flew around her head as if to crown her. Beside her was a water barrel, round and voluptuous, echoing the strength and shape of her hips. Beneath it, around it, were frogs with gleaming pink tongues, mouths open as if catching the morning whole. The heel of the iron was silver in the sunlight, her face, her eyes, facing it all.

The second painting he had called 'Martha in Marseilles', but rather she was in a meadow with a pail of mussels beside her. This time she wore clogs, her knees apart, a knife in her hand ready to scrape the shells. At her feet were oysters, open and gleaming, and yet around her a meadow, on what looked like a summer afternoon. There was wheat tangled with poppies, and corncrake and rue. No sense of a salt wind, or the tang of seaweed; just Martha's hand, empty, reaching out to him. She was not young, she was not beautiful, but Robert had made her more than that, not by changing or altering but by infusing the painting with longing. His longing so evident it was as if spilled into the meadow.

In the third painting, she was naked and lying in the grass, her breasts huge and pink, a vein emeraldy in the crook of her knee. Her skin was not smooth and taut but dimpled and fat, yet she was glorious, glorious, sprinkled in delphinium petals. On her throat, in her hair, on the turn of her foot, her body was stippled in petals of the deepest blue.

The fourth painting was a triptych he had called 'Martha as Siren'. It was painted on the seashore, and this time I was sure they had been there. There was something about the colour of the water, the way the wind had whipped up her skin. The first panel showed her on the beach, by a rock, dressed in a coat buttoned to the neck and wearing sturdy shoes. Her hair was blown by the breeze that must have come up from the water, the sky and the sea a fudge of blues and greens. In her hand was a clutch of round smooth pebbles, the pebbles outstretched as if in offering to him.

In the second panel, she had gained a fish tail, her legs gazumphed by silver and pink. A voluptuous, snaking, fabulous tail, tipped with flukes that lay on the sand. And scattered around the rock were the things of her everyday life. An iron, a cooking pot, a metal spoon. A mop, a broom, wooden pegs foamed by the spray. The pebbles in her hands now buttons, held out in her hand to him.

In the third panel she was mermaid entire; her face still recognisable in a bare-breasted body all fin.

Pink and silver and green, and the hand still out-stretched, and this time the buttons all turned to jewels, rubies and emeralds and fire-white opals. Martha, surrounded by the things she owned, the things they used, in the places they went to. Martha the plain. Martha the sumptuous. Martha made glorious by what he obviously felt.

What pained me when I first saw them, and in truth what still hurts my pride now, was that he had not dressed her like a seductress in the robes of a goddess. He had not given her a bow with which to vanquish me. Instead, mostly what she held was simply an iron; smoothing away me and everything I stood for.

I have not looked at these paintings for years, and now they are unfurled before me again. I am unsettled by Kate, by what she did not say. The same old mistakes all over again. Something about her, some echo of the same pain. Something I should teach her, but which I am unsure if I have properly learnt myself.

I think I must give these to Martha; I'm sure I can find out where she is. They are rightfully hers, I should never have kept them. Years in this cupboard, held rolled by my neat flat knots; they are hers, and his diary, and her book from the day of the funeral.

Somehow, I feel if I can give them to her I can make it all whole. I can tell Kate, if I am able, that things are sometimes not what they seem. I can try to tell her that sometimes there is a way back, and although not in my marriage, still wisdom to gain. I can try to give her fortitude in the face of whatever she is thinking. I can tell her that sometimes, unavoidably, love falls where it may.

I can see, mostly, that it is a question of spirit. A way of seeing, of comfortableness within one's own skin. These virtues were Martha's, were Martha's to give, and were the obverse of an object, they could not be held, be measured. Not like a reassuring weight, solid in one's palm.

Now, three days later I am outside an old people's home. This time, not laundry, but canvases and books in my hands. This time I am more fearful than that morning in June. Less, somehow, to lose, but a feeling that this is braver.

I wonder what she looks like; if she has diminished with age. Perhaps she is senile, and has no memory of it now. Perhaps she will look at the paintings and think they are of someone else; will read what he wrote and not remember it is about her. I do not want to stand before her and speak loudly, over-clearly, *Robert, remember Robert? These things belonged to him.*

In the foyer I stand beside a small glass fish tank, and watch a fish swimming through a blue plastic boat. How I hate these places. How I hope never to be somewhere like this; visiting hours and shiny smile voices, name tags in clothing or wearing someone else's blouse. I am horrified suddenly by the thought that Martha's eyes might be blue-empty,

98

her face nodding and bobbing in an overly warm dayroom.

I want her to have these things, but I understand suddenly, clearly, that I do not want to see her. I want only to remember her as she was in the paintings. *Always M. Only M.* radiant in a green dress, not shrivelled, collapsed, like a rotting fig.

And so I go to the woman at the reception desk and alter my request. I do not want to see Martha, I will simply leave her these things. I turn and leave, wondering for a moment what will become of them, but keep walking resolutely, knowing they are not mine, but theirs.

At home, I sit by my piano. I will play Chopin until my fingers ache. All these years later, I know what I see. Love and its absence. Familiarity. Longing. A knowledge of love, and the knowledge that it was not mine, and then living as if it were easy to do without.

There are things in my life that I can say I owned. Things in my life that belonged to me. An empty epitaph of things that do not endure. Martha's confidence, in contrast, still springs white hot from a canvas. In the face of all this, this is what I know. I have lived a life without substance. I have not used my heart. It is this I must change, and I will talk to my daughter.

CHAPTER 4

MARTHA

May ever remain in perfect love and peace

I was puzzled at first. I don't expect visitors, not visitors for me personally; the local school coming to sing to the whole Home, or the hairdresser on Thursdays to see who wants a comb-through or a set, but not anyone to see me, to sit in my room and talk to me. I don't say that in a mean-spirited or complaining way. Both my boys emigrated to Australia years ago, and are very good about sending letters and postcards, but it's a hardly a bus-trip, and my husband's been dead seven years now, long enough for any connexions there to fall away.

I'm not lonely or unhappy, I'm not short of company. I have a good friend, Rose (that's one of my discoveries about old age – the differences matter less and the similarities are easier to concentrate on.) We play whist and rummy and draughts, and when the weather is warm we walk in the garden and dead-head the flowers to keep them coming and talk of things we did and what we thought. Except about him. I don't talk about him.

Even though I can start the sound of him and the feel of him and the smell of him in my head and he's there so forcefully I'm giddy. A giddy old woman with reasonably good knees.

I don't usually go into the lobby – perhaps only to help one of the frailer ones to the chair in front of the fish tank. By the reception desk you can see straight out through the door to the step; I can't help but notice it hasn't been given a good scrub in years. My mother used to say, *There's more as passes by as comes in.* What a thing to saddle me with, years of scrubbing the step, washing down the paintwork and sweeping the path, as if it guaranteed the respectability within. Enough of a habit, though, for me to notice that this one needs doing, and the cobwebs fetching off from the top of the door frame, but I'm not tempted to ask for a bucket and do it myself, sleeves up, teeth gritted, watching for the transformation. No, the compulsion's long gone, it's just the memory that it mattered that's stayed. That's probably what it's like for most of the people in here; people they loved, things they did. They can remember that it mattered but it doesn't matter any more, and in that, a kind of worn-out peace.

And today, I'd only gone down there to find out if there was a whist drive tonight (someone had wandered off with the list on the notice board), when a woman came in through the door (cobweb now wafting up with the in-draught) and walked up to the reception desk and said my name; said it in a clear, well-spoken way that I felt I should have been able to place instantly. She was standing with her back to me. She wasn't stooped in the least – a spine and posture as straight as could be – but I could tell by her hair (grey and pinned into some kind of chignon) and by her shin bones that she was not quite my age but close. Usually, ordinarily, I would have walked up and touched her on the shoulder – I have nothing to fear from un-expected visitors – but something unsettled me, something made me turn on my heel and scoot, even though I was intrigued by what she was carrying. I could see books, rolls of something, something leather-bound – but it didn't occur to me they could be intended for me. No, at that point I thought it was probably some trivial mistake – perhaps an old church register enquiry, or maybe something to do with voting – and that what was in her arms was her business alone. But there was something, something hard to describe, like a feather brushed over the back of my hand, an echo, a reminder of something long back. I was suddenly sure that her face would be familiar to me, and there it was, her voice suddenly taking me back to my own front door, a summer morning, all those years ago, my knuckle in my mouth where I had caught it in the lock.

Back in my room, I sat down in my armchair and looked out of the window; tried to look absorbed in the tree branches tugged by the east wind, so that when there was a tap on the door

I could casually say, *Come in*, and at the same time, take a deep breath, my right hand blenched white from gripping the chair. When the knock came, it was only Jackie, the receptionist, carrying the armful of things.

'She asked me to give these to you', she said, 'she left no name'.

She laid them out on the bed, so that what I suddenly saw to be paintings started to unfurl, and then I knew, knew with a start that winded me, what it was, who she was, and what she had brought to me. And so, with Jackie out of the room, I sat with my head in my hands, heart pounding. After all these years, to be with his things in the same room again. Understanding still, as I understood then, that the whole point of my life was him. That Robert was the huge, explosive, fire-cracking, world-spinning point of it all.

When I was born in Oxfordshire in 1920, England was still raw from the war. All those flickering films of dancing flapper girls, and cars, and liners setting sail aren't it at all; instead, it was like holding your breath, knowing everything had changed. My mother's brother Albert died in 1916 walking across the Somme into a tangle of wire and gunfire. As a boy, he liked rabbiting, and that's how I always saw his death, like a rabbit snared in wire, snagged, eyes wide open. His photograph was on the wall above the kitchen table, smiling self-consciously from beneath his corporal's hat, set to make something of himself but with no chance at all.

103

I was not a beautiful child nor a beautiful woman. I was solid and strong like a wide-armed chair; broad-beamed, broad-busted, with thick ankles and lardy arms. Slabs of flesh that denied the bones beneath; not wobbly, just a body that was designed to carry things, fold sheets, iron shirts, pull pints, carry children. A body made for work when my mother dreamed of a flower fairy.

In my house, I understood from the off that cleanliness was next to Godliness and that nothing pleased Jesus more than clean hands, a clean nose, and a well-eaten dinner. My mother standing me on the table, socks peeled down to my ankles, scrubbing me with the flannel until I was rosy-kneed. In Bible lessons, hoping it was as simple to get your insides scrubbed. Chanting the Thanksgiving *'Give thee most humble and hearty thanks for all thy goodness and loving-kindness . . . and all the blessings of this life . . . we show forth thy praise, not only with our lips but with our lives'* and wondering if this meant walking quietly past Tom Price who had the shakes from the war and lived with his mother again; a man-child now, my mother said, who was no longer right in the head, as if the rest of him was right enough. His mother back with a toddler, steering him down the street away from front doors that slammed. Maudie Taylor, the big, stout Catholic who lived three doors along telling her to *Offer it up, offer it up,* as if somehow that would make it right. The notion that the body belonged to God and best not question.

When I started my periods, and pieced all that business together from what my mother and Maudie told me, I thought suddenly of the Virgin Mary, and all those nativity paintings with her smiling serenely in the stable, blue and white and composed, star twinkling overhead, and ox and asses and shepherd boys with flutes, and realised that she probably wasn't feeling serene at all, but bloody and sticky, and the ride on the donkey making her bladder ache. Maudie telling me that Jesus was made through Mary's ear, and wondering how that had worked, and thinking for the first time that maybe the Bible didn't tell you it all, or that maybe God had different rules depending on who you were.

I'd sit at Maudie's to escape our kitchen all steamed up with dinner, and she'd let me hold her rosary; amethyst beads in a special order, starting with a silver Jesus on a silver cross. A cross, then a single bead up from the cross, then three beads, then one more. An oval disc of silver engraved with an M, then a cross, then two hearts, one with a dagger through it and one with twelve little stars all around. And then Mary on the other side, hands outstretched as if she wouldn't mind to pick you up even if you were grubby, and more words: *O Mary conceived without sin pray for us who have recourse to thee.* Then Jesus on the cross, with the nails through his hands, and the line of his ribs, and his muscles all clear, even his belly button. A scroll nailed to the cross, but I couldn't make out the letters on it. Lord? Ecce? And on the back, in capital letters I-T-A-L-Y. I'd sit on Maudie's lap while she said it, first the Apostles' Creed, then Our Father, three Hail Marys and then Glory be to the Father.

There were five mysteries; joyful ones and sorrowful ones and glorious ones. I liked that; that Maudie could take the rosary and follow the same route and make it happy or sad; filled with peace and blessings or agony and scourging and grand things that started with The. The Resurrection. The Assumption. The Ascension. The Coronation. Sitting on Maudie's fat broad lap with the beads between my finger and thumb, listening to her say all the words and wishing that it could be like that in life; see the route mapped out, the footprints there and then choose the style of it. See the whole, and understand better.

But then, just Maudie's words and her smell of soap and cabbage and starch, and her skin all papery soft, and wispy bits of hair stuck to her neck with steam or sweat. Over the mantelpiece a picture of Jesus, watching us, head tilted on one side, his eyes all weary with a halo yellow as an egg yolk. Maudie called the picture 'Jesus in need of a good sit down which was not surprising when you think of all he had to do'.

Dad tanning me when he caught me making a rosary with white stones in the yard, complaining to my mother that Maudie was filling my head with papist nonsense. My mother saying it was no different from or worse than anything else that might be in there. Not that any of it saved me or stopped me in the end. Having knowledge of what not to do but doing it all the same. And once, when Maudie's back was turned cleaning out the coal scuttle, just quickly putting the rosary into my mouth and sucking it to see what it was like; whether it made you feel different inside. But not; just cold and hard and bobbly, like sucking pebbles. Not like the bread and wine magic that Maudie explained to me – that sounded something – wine into blood right there in your mouth. Warm and thick and sweet, and the bread into his body. *Isn't that like eating Jesus?* I asked her. She stopped scrubbing. Thought. *In a way, I suppose.* And I understood, years later, the wish to consume. To carry love around, inside of you. Precious, unspillable, blood-red bright.

As a young girl, sitting with Pearl Armstrong on the wall at the end of the street, singing, *The gypsy rover came over the hill, down through the valley so shady. He whistled and he sang until the greenwoods rang, and he won the heart of his lady.* Wondering what it would be like for me. Whether someone would whistle and sing until the greenwoods rang and that would be me all accounted for. Impossible to imagine, forty-three years later, a man in a churchyard with a book.

When I was seventeen I worked in Mrs Trewitt's shoe shop in the town. You can tell a lot by a person's shoes, Mrs Trewitt used to say, and even more by their feet, as if chilblains and bunions came only to the guilty.

Bill was a plumber, doing his apprenticeship with Mr Stafford. They came to put a basin in at the back of the shop. Mrs Trewitt trilling around; wanting customers to know that we stretched to modern facilities but not wanting plumbers' bags on the good wool carpet. *It's the grease*, she said later, *it gets everywhere*.

The first time I clapped eyes on Bill, I watched him standing there passing bits of piping to Mr Stafford, not saying much, rootling around in the brown leather bag. Broad shouldered, with a sinewy neck and big wide hands and blue eyes with no sparks of cleverness but kind. Noticing he was looking me up and down. Silently. Approvingly. As if he could put a washer on me and have me fixed up in no time. And because there were no customers – it was late on a Wednesday afternoon – watching him clean and wipe all the tools and put them away. For the first time, the litany that would run through the years. Bill's big broad thumbs smoothing and checking and wiping each coppery tube, each silver spanner; his rosary of the plumbing bag, each thing in its right place, a language of interlocking parts.

Dressing that Friday night, ready for him to come and meet me. I was dressed in blue, a dress that wrapped across the front of me and fell in soft folds. Neat shoes. Lipstick. Hair in some semblance of order. My mother in her chair in the kitchen, saying, *You look grand*, encouragingly if a little doubtfully. You all have your bouquets to offer, she used to say to us, although perhaps a little stumped to say what mine might have been. Buxom. Good-hearted. Always dreaming of words. Could that be counted as a bouquet? I would like to tell her that at fifty-eight I had bouquets enough to fill a whole flower shop. Armfuls and armfuls of myself to give. Bouquets I never even knew I had. There are pears that only ripen in December; that's what I'd like to tell her now.

Bill at the door all nervous and shy. At the dance, dancing together hesitantly. The valves no longer in his fingers but twisting them anyway. The solidness of his body; the thick scratchiness of his wool jacket against my cheek, a faint smell of wardrobes, of clothes that didn't get out in the air much. The smell of soap along the top of his collar. My husband, all scrubbed up; knowing that already, and although not excitement in that knowledge, peace.

We married at St James' Church, in new shoes given by Mrs Trewitt. Mine were little buff kitten heels with a strap across the instep; a neat button to fasten it up, and my foot surprised in a cream stocking. It's odd that I can see those still, and yet not remember my wedding night. The cake, made by Mrs Coleman from the Albert Road. White stiff little rosebuds, all around the edge, and cutting it with Bill and saying, *Remember, we mustn't cut through to the bottom, it's bad luck*, and

Bill saying, *As if a cake cut could change the flow of things*. As if indeed.

Our first house, in fact our only house, was rented on Porter Street and bought years later. It was at the end of a terrace, with a path running up the side of it, past the front door and round to the back. Next to the back door, a rain barrel, balanced on four bricks to catch the rain and the overflow. Through the back door into the kitchen; a small fireplace with tiles round it and a black grate. *That will be easy to keep clean*, my mother said, *not much to black*. Her way of measuring and at that time, mine too. Cleanliness as next to Godliness. Then.

A small parlour. Two armchairs bought second hand from Manny Solomon. Brick red, with wings at the head and big broad arms. He laughed when I sat in it. *Martha Fraser, that chair was made with your limbs in mind*. Not in I-T-A-L-Y. Not exotic. Probably in Leeds or somewhere.

Two rooms upstairs, a privy up the garden path outside. Years later, Bill plumbing it all inside. Two pig sties at the bottom of the garden, then the steep escarpment made by the railway line. Years and years of lying in bed and hearing the trains go by. In the winter, making me press down deeper into the blankets, cosier at the thought, and in the summer, making me restless, thinking of others travelling, visiting, seeing things I wouldn't. Starting a wanderlust that peppered my sleep but dissolved in the morning when the shirts came for ironing. The feeling that the ironing board was

110

rooted into the ground and that all the hours I stood there, my feet grew roots too, deep into the floor. My arms like branches up from the ironing board. Solidly smoothing. The thought, especially during the war, that what the world needed was a good ironing. That God obviously didn't get involved with creases.

Married life with Bill straightforward from the off. His view that in this life much of what was said was probably better left unsaid, and much of what was left was probably just rattle, so better silent. Comfortable quietness. Like the ox and the ass; peaceful, companionable. All those years to have never seen him naked, nor him me. Modesty tied up with limited expectations. Just coupling; quietly, peacefully, in the dark.

In 1940, a year after we were married, growing rounder and soldier still. Bold about my new outline, knowing there was room enough in me for all of this, and loving the swooshing kicks inside. Birthing like an old hand, with Rose Black to help. You'd think you'd had four already, she said. Four pushes and a slithery swoop and a wet little mop head and screwed up fingers and a round O mouth yelling fit to bust. Putting him to me to feed; propped up on the pillow like a pink fat sow. Automatic. Instinctive. Simple.

Bill coming upstairs after Rose had gone; thumb pad circling the edge of his opposite cuff, as if somehow surprised that I'd done it for him. Looking at his son, and holding him carefully, the baby's fist in the curl of his finger. We called him John; and in 1942, another one, Peter. Keep it simple. Fishers of men names.

I loved the boys, loved them up; their pudgy toddler limbs, and then little boy legs. Their wet-bright eyes, and naughtiness and muddiness. The smell of them after a bath. The look of them asleep in flannelette striped pyjamas. Their short cropped hair and the shape of their foreheads. The bits of rubbish in their pockets at the end of the day; the ant homes, worm tunnels and mole traps dug in the back yard. But not changed by it, not becoming Martha, patient saint of mothering, arms outstretched. Not becoming Maudie either, talking and working and talking some more, always ready to stop and lift you onto her lap and tell you something. Instead, too much *Out from under my feet* from me, swooshing the broom behind them.

Then, when the boys were getting bigger, doing cleaning for three houses; sorting other peoples' messes. Seeing straight through some fancy ways, but liking the feel of nice things. Chinese lamps, soft throws over armchairs, mahogany sideboards with handles inlaid with mother of pearl, Persian rugs made from coloured thread I didn't have words to name, beds with coverlets made from old French lace. One made from crushed velvet with crystal droplets at the edge that chinked softly when I did the corners. Welsh dressers stacked with good china. Crystal glasses that rang when I touched them.

Woollen coats with cashmere in them. Soft to the fingers.

I worked lunchtimes and three evenings in the Working Men's Club in Bower Street. Pulling pints and tidying up; nearly all men in there, but most not working. Boozing. Talking. Using words but not giving anything away. Sorrows and lost hopes swaddled up in beer and fags. Only their eyes showing their innards when the drink peeled their guard away, uncertain boy faces peeping back out, wanting their mam, for an instant. Slumped tired old faces with no resolve left. The smell of the beer; the line of their shoulder blades. Adrift of their anchor, nothing to do making them feel like nothing. But not saying. Watching some of them come in strutting like little bantams; full of the crack and bantering to me. *Martha my lovely, Martha my darling*. And later, mopping out the toilets, thinking if they learnt to aim straight we might move the world on a little.

At chucking out time, helping to pick up the ones who'd had a skinful; pulling them up by the elbow, sending them on their way, onto their feet and out of the door. The night air bracing, and making them snort in their next breath, eyes blinking. Martha the handmaiden, and while they were not recognisably Maudie's Jesus, Him probably in there somewhere. And if they started spoiling for a fight, jollying them out if it; nudging them back from their boxer's stance with a hand on their arm. Looking a bit blowsy myself probably; lipstick too

113

red, busty barmaid, but more like their mother. Chiding them home to bed and then emptying the ashtrays. Remembering *Blessed are the peacemakers* and thinking perhaps He missed something out. The picker-uppers. The mainly women. The putters to rights. Smoothing, folding, restoring, soothing, cleaning, wiping snot. Getting on with it.

When I came home from working Saturday lunchtime, Bill would be out by the sty with the pigs. Two huge pink Tamworth sows with coarse ginger hair on their backs. I would always find him there, scratching their backs, watching them shift and rootle as he collected apples for their trough from the crab tree on the escarpment in an old black bucket with a split handle. Using the same bucket to carry water up from the rain barrel. And always quiet. The odd word to them. Pushing them with his legs when he shovelled out the manure, their soft rubbery snouts snuffling. The scrunch of the apples. The water slopping over the sides of the water trough. Their trotters black and shiny like mussel shells, neat against the floor of the sty. Wafting drowsy flies away with my hand, leaning over the sty wall. My behind probably looking much like theirs. Flat. Broad. Slappable. Asking him about his day. *Aye*. If he'd sorted the pumping on Mrs Chapman's shower. And not ask more. Not rattle. Just stand, companionably, not me not needing words but him not choosing them. And I wondered if he would have been happier doing this, farming stock, tending to cattle. Walking over fields ploughed to chocolate ripples. Breath to mist on a frosty morning. And asking him, once, if that would have been better than the pipes and u-bends and joints and pumps. The sentence hanging thinly between us. And him saying, jaw down, that most times, folk get the life they would choose. And thinking it true; that if he'd said yes, I couldn't really have seen him striding out, legs planted wide over a furrow, rustling wheat through his hand to see if it was ripe. The pigs one thing, but the litany of his plumbing bag his real peace. Each pipe in its place. Each valve properly greased. Each spanner according to size. The neatness of it. Not done in the face of what he saw beyond it, but because it was good in itself. Separate. Self-sufficient. Like him really. A good man, whose version of love was decent behaviour and companionship.

On a Sunday morning, he'd go off to the canal, fishing. Get up early, make a bacon sandwich to take, sometimes catching, sometimes not. A few perch, or a roach, carefully put back. Sitting on a folding blue stool he kept under the stairs; a brown canvas bag with his hooks and bait. On winter mornings his cap pulled down low. Telling me, sometimes, things he had seen; that the water looked oily, the heron on the bridge again. And in the afternoon, digging in his allotment; carrots and cabbages and runner beans. Potatoes, marrows, sometimes peas; all in neat rows, a few marigolds between. His shed at the end and an old deck chair. I'd go down there sometimes to get some vegetables for dinner. The potatoes always floury but neither of us saying.

And when he came in to eat, we'd sit next to each other at the blue and white Formica table. Modern and wipeable, no need for scrubbing. The cutlery thin and awkward in his big hands. It made me think of the pigs in the sty, chewing quietly side by side. Not the company of strangers. The strangeness of company.

My mother died, of a stroke that first made her left side limp and useless. Mouth battling to chew or talk; being dressed, washed. Knowing how much she hated it; how much she would have liked to spring up from the bed and flannel herself clean as if dirty from a coal mine. Lazarus all over. To have scrubbed and cleaned and purged away her uselessness; clean before God and ready to give the step before St Peter's gate a good going over. The last time I saw her, sitting by the bed and holding her better hand. No wisdom to impart; me still baffled by what she had expected me to be; her still baffled by a world you couldn't clean up. Me about to explode every notion of respectability she ever taught me. Her clutching the sheet edge, wet-eyed with the indignity of the bed pan.

Maudie too; gone for a good sit down. At her funeral the air thick with incense, sweet and cloying and exotic. Like I-T-A-L-Y. Her rosary in the coffin with her, worn smooth with all the handling; Jesus's ribs not quite so defined.

116

Afterwards, going to her house and helping with the sorting of things. Asking, if no-one wanted it, if I could have Jesus with the egg yolk halo, Jesus with the weary eyes. Taking it home and putting it in the bedroom, and Bill asking where it had come from, and what would I be wanting with that, and not replying properly; not saying that this was how my Jesus looked.

John and Peter both marrying, and having children. All that cuddling up, all over again. Sitting with one of the grandchildren on my lap, going through my button tin. Gold buttons with anchors on. Square buttons with sparkly glass centres, sapphire blue diamond shapes, polished and shiny. Maple toggles, etched frosted glass. Jiggling them in clasped hands, and sifting them through fingers. Flashes of colour and a whooshing, clinking noise. Little voices chanting, legs swinging from my lap. *Rich man poor man beggar man thief.* Singing to them softly; *A frog he did a wooing go.* And then Robert.

On a Wednesday, aged fifty-eight, waiting for the bus, and not sat at the bus stop, because the rain puddled there and the cars splashed it up, so sitting in the churchyard opposite, on a broad beamed bench with the shopping at my feet, able to see over the low dry stone wall if the bus was coming.

The churchyard always quiet. Sitting amongst the dead, watching a robin sing from the top of a gravestone. The moss bright green and frizzled and curled at the edges of the stones; the lettering

117

filled with lichen, dark green and yellow. I never felt morbid sitting there; soothed somehow. That all the chasing around and fetching and carrying finally came to this. All the rattle reduced to one robin's song and a shaft of sunlight cutting across a stone; to some sparse words, and maybe a cross and a date to fix you in the pattern of it all.

That day, just enjoying the spring flowers; Aubretia and Alyssum scrambling out of the wall, and Pasque flowers with silky seedheads and late Primulas in the dappled shade and beautiful blue Veronica. Veronica, she interested me too. Maudie had told me the story of her handkerchief, and the imprint His face left on it when she wiped His brow. Veronica, another of the picker-uppers; the wipers and cleaners. Finding it astonishing that you could touch Him and carry away an imprint, see His features in a handkerchief. And that day, about to understand that it could happen. That you could be imprinted upon. That you could touch someone and walk away, not with their features on cloth, but on you. Imprinted on you and in you. Right to the bone.

But on that day, just looking at the flowers, listening to the robin, and feeling the warmth of the spring sunshine across my knees. Thinking how nice it was to have warm knees, and thinking of long-ago fine ladies in grand carriages with rugs across their laps and hair piled-up in elaborate styles, and chalk white skin and footmen riding behind. Then, catching in the corner of my eye the sight of a man standing to the east of the church with a book in his hand looking up at the roof. Watching, despite myself, as he walked around, all the time looking and turning the pages in his book. Knowing straight away that he wasn't the type to be drinking at Bower Street; the jacket a soft tweed with bluey heathery greens, his shoulder blades too composed, his shoes too fine. The book too accustomed in his hands. His skin warm from the soft freshness of a spring day, not weather-beaten and whipped from working outside. Noticing with a start that he was looking right back, and wondering what he thought he saw. Maybe a middle-aged woman with thick ankles on a broad beamed bench with shopping at her feet. Wondering why the thought occurred to me; long past the time when men held any mysteries. Or so I thought.

Puzzled as to what I wanted him to see, this well-dressed man with a book in a churchyard on a day in May with a robin singing and the number fifteen bus late again. Wondering why I didn't look away, and why I was smiling back. As he walked towards me, resisting the urge to move along on the bench which would have openly invited him to sit awhile, and at the same time seeing the bus coming around the corner, and not standing up, not moving at all, but instead sitting quite still and watching him walk towards me with a book in one hand and his other hand empty except that it held the rest of my life.

A saddleback roof, he said. A brilliant example

of a saddleback roof; showing me in his book, his index finger pressing the page open, a drawing of a saddleback roof. The half moon on the nail of his finger white, clean and even. A brown leather button on the cuff of his jacket, stitched into quarters and resting on the edge of the page. And me looking up, looking up at the roof of the church to paste a name on it. To learn, then, that a saddleback roof is a tower roof shaped like a gabled timber roof, and asking him what other sorts there were. Waggon roofs with close-set rafters and arched braces. Hipped roofs. Tie-beam roofs. A whole new litany. Roofs made from ridges, common rafters, principal rafters, king posts, purlins, queen posts, struts, collar beams and hammer beams. Roofs that kept the rain out and lifted the eyes up to God. A rosary of roofs.

There's a bellcote, he said, on the west side. Bellcote another new word; a tower for bells that made me think of birds, with white dove notes flying out of it. Standing and walking with him towards the bellcote, past a window with a wedge shaped stone at the top, and asking him if that had a name. Hungry for his words. A voussoir. Liking that too. Like boudoir and slippery softness and feather cushions and round mouths. A word that sounded like it was asking you to do something, rather than naming a stone. Do you voussoir? Yes, voussoir me.

We turned to each other by a lilac tree, a white lilac tree in a packet of its own perfume, and his words tripping and falling between the branches, and me looking at him, and knowing desire, and longing, for the first time, at my age. And knowing too that it was not just desire. It was the pulse of all the words not yet said. All the things not yet shared. The feeling, for the first time, of being an interlocking part; sliding into each other with a small click beneath the lilac tree. And still not moving; some more brief words. Where he lived. Where I lived. That he had a wife. That I had a husband. That he was a GP. That I ironed clothes. Telling me where his surgery was; doctoring the villages on the edge of town. And me thinking that he would have a bag too; a bag with stethoscopes, thermometers, antibiotics, bandages. Human plumbing. Him saying that he loved churches, church architecture, and visiting churchyards with his book, each Wednesday afternoon when he had no surgery. Finding roll moulding and finials and fillets and spirelets. Tapping walls to see if they were made of cob – clay mixed with straw from long ago harvests. I liked that thought too. Seeing a long-ago hot day in July and a scythe cutting grass, and a man's hands tying the grass into bundles and drying it in a barn and mixing it with clay and slapping and patting it into a wall. All is safely gathered in and made into churches; liking the neatness of that, the circle, and a man, now, who tapped walls to find it.

Standing before him, fixing his shape in my eye. His height, the breadth of his shoulders, the lines on his forehead, the lines around his eyes. His hair thick and grey-white, his eyebrows with some dark in them. Blue eyes; paint-chart blue eyes. Clear and clean. Eyes filled with looking at me too; tiny versions of myself in his pupils, spinning down, down into his bottomless eyes. Not drowning. Skydiving. My lark time. Agreeing to meet him there next Wednesday.

I went home and peeled the potatoes for tea. Stood at the sink scraping the skin into the colander; cutting them into quarters; sealing the meat in the frying pan. Looked out of the window and saw a cloud so thick you could take a bite out of it. Plugged in the iron, ready to start Mrs Collins' basket. Trying to start the tune of the evening, the rhythm of the house. The familiarity of things in my hands; the handle of the frying pan, the plug of the iron. The tipping of the potato skins into the pigs' bowl. Going outside to sit on the step, resting my head against the rain barrel, pressing my thumb nail into the moss at the edge. Crescent moons in the moss. Beginnings.

Knowing this, as I sat there, pressing the rust flakes onto my fingertips, knowing that I would have sat on the churchyard bench from that moment until next Wednesday just to see him again. Sat there like a fool in the spring rain and shine. Sat there for a week, just to look at the turn of his neck, at the inside of his wrist, at the line of his mouth. To imprint him. Be imprinted. Again.

Before I went to meet him the next week, I sat on

the side of the bed, looked at my painting of Jesus in need of a good sit down, feeling aware of my almost old, jiggle-jaggled body. The heaviness of my breasts, the snaky vein on my calf, the coarse skin on my elbows. Suddenly summoning Mrs Trewitt up before me. Remembering her telling me – she must have been in her fifties then too – that the best thing for elbows was to halve a lemon, remove the fruit and sit with your elbows in the halves. The pith and rind whitening and softening. And wondering who she'd been keeping her elbows nice for. What part of the week was deemed Care of Elbows. What other bits she had remedies for. What other things I might have learned. Seeing my mother suddenly. Apportioning to her mouth the flesh from Mrs Trewitt's lemon so that she could assume her sour mouth look and tell me I was fast, with ideas beyond myself. A doctor indeed. Married. And feeling all that fall away, like the thick spiky case from a horse chestnut, leaving me with a polished, gleaming, suckable conker, perfect in the palm of my hand. Feeling the quiet inter-locking click in the churchyard, beyond all of it. Knowing that I would talk to him, listen to him, love him. Knowing already that what Robert wanted in me, saw in me, Bill didn't even know was there.

Passion and rattle. Realising that whatever happened between Robert and me, nothing would change for Bill. The order of his day. His tea on the blue Formica table when he came home from work. Playing darts in The Crown for the league. Fishing in the canal on Sundays. All that would not change; I would keep all this from him; never justify it, but do it all the same. Knowing that what I was doing was by all notions wrong. Adulterous. Dishonest. But beyond all that, right. More right than anything had ever been for me. And I could spend the rest of my life wishing that I had met Robert when I was twenty, and watched him pack his bag through the years. But that I would not, I would not think of the whys and wherefores again. Instead, step off the bus and walk to the churchyard. Trembling.

Finding him waiting for me, through the arch of the lych gate, standing by a small stone angel. The angel with its eyes up; him with his eyes down, and then looking. Seeing me, and smiling as I walked towards him, my hands completely empty, just carrying myself, to him.

That first day we went for a walk, across the road from the church and onto a track that led across the fields. That track still so clear in my mind; now, at eighty-two, I can still see it unrolling before us, fixed forever on a day in May. White and green. The hawthorn covered in tiny white flowers, the stems and leaves so vivid. The cow parsley like white soft lace against the hedgerow. A hare starting and running, twisting away in front of us. A small patch of dark fur visible on its cheek; liquid eyes; all legs and feet.

I asked him why he loved churches, why he spent

afternoons seeking out spires and altars and stoups, whether to see God more clearly, or to understand man better; whether he was brought to church by God, or by men's God-buildings. By what man's hands could do, given a nudge in the right direction. *I will lift up mine eyes unto the hills from whence cometh my help.* And asking him how he saw his Jesus, in the face of his doctoring, people no hand could save. Not his, or His. Wondering where that left you; perhaps just liking the stones. Robert pausing, pressing a tuft of grass with his shoe, and agreeing that whatever God did like, he didn't mind creases. Creases that couldn't be ironed and steamed out with any amount of goodness. Creases that resisted any explanation, any fairness. Churches, he thought, simpler somehow. Men aiming to the good. Crocketing the sloping side of a spire with tumbling leaf shapes. Making cupolas to crown roofs. Making cartouches and lancet windows. In the face of it all. And the face of it all sometimes so beautiful it could make you trip. A track in May all white and green; a hare bolting through cow parsley.

Later, foreheads pressed together, as if breathing each other in. His hands holding my face, as if something precious, found. I have been waiting for you, he said, for so very very long. Not answering him, but feeling it too. Back in the churchyard, reaching into his pocket and bringing out a wrapped gift. A book, A *Guide to English Parish Churches*, the same as his. I thought you might like it, he said, we could go together, on Wednesdays.

And so it began. Walking around churchyards on Wednesdays. Churches made of flintstone, of Cotswold stone, of marlstone, of redbrick. Looking at steeples and arches and carvings and tracery and chancels, and mullions soaring from floor to ceiling. Always talking; all the things never said, never shared, until then. Sometimes silent, sitting back to back, looking at carvings; self-satisfied knights in effigy, weepers on the side of tombs, a tree of Jesse made of glass and stone. And loving the words. Spandrels and corbels and ogees and cinquefoil canopies; trying them out in my mouth. Words that made me think of pieces of jewellery; ornate brooches stuck onto medieval clothing, words that carried the centuries along before them. Not like my workaday, everyday words; the church words winking and flashing like jewels. Robert smiling and calling me a wordcomber, picking up words like sticks on a beach and carrying them home to keep.

Loving him, the first time, in a small hotel in the Cotswolds; an afternoon in June with the air soft to the skin; ravenous for each other. Learning his outline, his shape, his smell, and feeling my own body, tumbling and moving and loosening like water, and understanding for the first time, the whole point of it all. The reason for all the fuss. The whole room-spinning, skin-melting point of it all. And all the time looking into his blue eyes, my naked body smaller and smaller, blurring the line of where he stopped and I started. The moment under the lilac tree, given flesh. And afterwards, laughing, that this unbelievable redemption might be ours. Then, just holding each other. You mean everything, he said, and me unable to speak for tears. Inside, for the first time, so alive.

Little stories, that's what we made up; little slices of life, together. Sharing the feeling that the truth of it, and the weight of it, was in the detail. That your whole life could be caught in the little things. Looking at the gravestone of a long-ago child who died aged twelve. Imagining the sampler she might have sewn, jabbing away at her stitches and pricking her finger, raising her stiff neck to look out of the window at a child with a hoop outside. Feeling at odds with her tiny embroidered flowers, the biblical verse, her finger with its bubble of blood; yeasty dough rising on the range beside her.

Or, looking at a gargoyle and wondering who carved it. Whether a child came skipping to bring the stonemason lunch while he worked, bread and cheese, or cold pigeon pie. Whether he had a chair before his fire, a pile of cherry wood in the grate. Whether an old leghorn rooster crowed in his yard.

A year after we met, lying in a cornfield under a blazing June sky. A skylark visible above through the web of my lashes, wheeling and soaring and singing, and Robert taking from his pocket a handful of delphinium petals, the bluest of blue. *Last night in the garden, I wanted them for you.*

127

And he scattered them over me, over my breasts, my arms, into my hair. Lying there, the green of the corn, the whip-thin poppy stems, the blue of the sky, and the petals all over me, making my bones sing new. That night, at home, undressing, finding one last petal tucked inside my clothes. Quickly concealing it in my closed hand, catching and holding the afternoon and all that brightness, and putting it under my pillow to savour in sleep. Thinking that when I am dead, if a couple, quietly talking in a churchyard made a story of my life, they would never guess that I slept on a delphinium petal pillow, warm from my breast, scattered from my lover's hand.

Once, at an agricultural show on a hot day in July, inside a Horticultural Society tent. A vegetable competition, all the categories marked with neat, clear signs. *Five potatoes, kidney or oval; twelve shallots for pickling; three carrots, long.* Marmalade jars, chutney jars, Victoria sponges made to a specified recipe. Isobel would like this, he said, this is Isobel's sort of tent. In his voice, somehow, the nearest he ever came to criticising her, not that I was hungry for him to do so. Mostly, we avoided mentioning either Bill or Isobel; avoiding explanation, motive, reasons why. Creating, instead, a world in which there were only the two of us, unfettered, free. Afterwards, sitting on a hay bale eating vension sausages in a roll and watching show jumping; betting with each other who would sail clear, who would fall. Like two old Gods on a mountain top, he said. Unaccountable. Safe.

Outside an old abbey in summer rain, getting wetter and wetter and finally going into a small gallery alongside. Watercolours of landscapes, of boats on waterfronts, fruit on kitchen tables, and then an empty eggshell so fine, so scooped clean, so perfect. Watching Robert look at it, and suddenly, uncontrollably, achingly wanting him. Then, in the car, the seat flipped back, the wheel pressed into my hips. The windows steaming up around us, the smell of wet clothes, warm rain. Kissing each other and murmuring into his skin, feeling my heart might stop with the joy of it.

On another afternoon, hiring a boat on a still, warm day; the water green and smooth, the banks a tangle of wetness. Robert moored the boat to an old wooden jetty, and we lay in a meadow bright with corncockle and rue. Robert took out a paint book and sketch pad; *A present from Kate*, he said, *I want to paint you.* So I sat, patient, unkempt, in the grass, my back straight, my feet planted wide, the sun warm on my face. *I feel*, I told him, *as if I should be wearing clogs, sitting on a stool in a harbour, a bucket of mussels at my feet with an old wooden knife with a small silver blade in my hand, scraping and cleaning the mussels.* All the time, looking straight at him, so bold, so emboldened. *So that's how I shall paint you*, he said. Simple as that.

Later, getting out of the car at the bottom of the street and walking up to the house, knowing

Bill would be home. Straightening and tugging at my dress, at my hair. Putting to rights. Yet feeling as if trailing corncockle and rue; feeling ravished, pink with fulfilment, like a fat cat with the cream. Making the tea in the kitchen, hard-boiled eggs and pickle, tomatoes cut in half on a lettuce leaf. And all the time, my heart singing and soaring; still legs akimbo, with him.

One morning, the phone ringing, then a neat careful voice, a woman's voice that was not familiar to me, explaining that her housekeeper was on holiday and could she drop off some shirts. Such a beautiful day I decided I would iron outside, the breeze already warm, the honeysuckle alive with bees, the livingstone daisies open to the sun. Robert laughed when I told him I did this. Told me he'd painted me ankle deep in grass and butterflies, ironing by the rain barrel. 'Aphrodite Ironing' he'd called it.

She knocked at the front door which took me by surprise. A front door was for policemen, for balliffs, for coffins; everyone else came round the back. I went to the door and started to undo it; the bolt all stiff, the frame a little swollen, and scrabbled for the key in the rose jug on the mantelpiece. All the time I was trying to open it, hearing her feet shift on the step, and a small cough, and the sound of car keys in her hand. And as I finally yanked the bolt across, pulling with my left hand whilst pressing down with my right, I caught my finger and pinched it badly, so opening the door with my knuckle in my mouth.

Nothing remarkable. Or at least not at that moment. My eye taking in a woman roughly my age, a little younger, neat and slim, with greying hair in a pleat held in place with a comb. Probably about my height, but looking smaller, with her standing one step down and me on the stoop. Aware that she was looking at me, really looking at me, but saying nothing, and me thinking I probably looked a sight, standing there sucking my finger, wanting to cuss but thinking probably better not. Clearing her throat to speak, but still saying nothing, just stretching out her hand and passing me the bag. I noticed that her nails were nice, polished and smooth, and that she wore a ring with a row of emeralds. Thinking that her usual ironer did a good job, because she was wearing a white blouse with an intricately stitched collar, and it was all done beautifully. Noticing her blouse, even while she told me that her house-keeper would be round to collect the shirts the day after tomorrow. Her voice even and clear, but with a tremble at the back, and me still thinking nothing of it.

Then, taking the ironing board out into the garden, and snapping up the wooden clothes horse to hang the coathangers on when they were done, and putting my hand in the bag and pulling out a plain white shirt. Thick, soft cotton with good buttons; somehow familiar to my touch. Then, a blue shirt with a double cuff with two pleats and a double split yoke, and suddenly knowing, suddenly seeing it, unbuttoned from Robert's body, my hands hungry for his skin. My first thought, his shirt on my ironing board some sort of gift. Not meant, but a gift all the same; the touch of it, the feel of it, holding what would hold him. Kissing the length of each seam, the circle of the collar, the turn of the cuff and each of the buttons. Thinking that when he stood in his bedroom and got dressed, I would be loving him. My garden kisses all over his shirt and brushed onto his skin.

Aware too, how apt it all was. Martha the ironing woman finally ironing his shirts. Of all the clothes that had passed through my hands, all the fabric I had touched and smoothed, to be finally touching his. To do what I did well, however little the task, to do it for him. Aware too, that an act so small could make my heart sing. Knowing that it couldn't always be like that; not every day, every cup you washed or every bed you made; but that suddenly, unexpectedly, the everyday rose up and became sacred. At that moment, in the garden, with a blue shirt hanging on a clothes horse and stirring softly in the breeze, I had been given a gift, unintentionally, but a gift all the same.

Later, when eight shirts were hanging up, I sat on the step with my tea and wondered what Isobel would do. Had she meant to challenge me, right there on the doorstep. *Do you know my husband, do you love my husband?* But seeing that was not in her eye, in the fixedness of her gaze. Perhaps it had been; perhaps it was her intention, but then unbelieving; surprised that he could love me, could want a woman like me. Perhaps baffled by my plainness, standing on a step sucking my knuckle. That he might want this. Aware too, that I would not have known how to answer her; a denial transparent, a confession vicious. And mindful of Bill; the thought that I had justified my silence and my faithlessness by keeping his world as he wanted it. Or seemed to want it. Shut calm tight and peaceful; the familiarity of me, the order of our days. The thought that Isobel might crack that all open for him; and then thinking damn her, why didn't she say something to Robert. Why come to me, on my doorstep, armed with knowledge in her perfect white blouse?

After telling Robert, both waiting to see what she would do next. Her housekeeper coming to collect the shirts, instinctively round to the back. Taking the shirts away, the sleeves flapping down the path. Pulling at my chest. And still no word. No word at their dinner table, no word in their bed, no question on her lips, no accusation in her eyes. Nothing. Like waiting for a storm that does not come. Waiting for the birds to go quiet and still. Waiting for the sky to turn leaden and blue, for the light to slice silvery and bruised. But not.

Is she different? I asked. *Has anything changed?* I asked.

No, nothing, he said, like a man somewhat at sea. *Nothing, nothing has changed.*

A week later, suddenly, understanding it all. The purpose of her visit not to shake up, to spill it all out and make us admit, but to put a face to her knowledge of me, to increase the sum of her understanding. And in the midst of all that she had simply not conceived, not thought I would know they were his shirts by touch, by memory, by the sex of it all. Not think that I would know it was her, not anonymous at all.

Yet, realising that I did not know what she felt at all. Perhaps that she saw Robert's clothes as I saw Bill's – things to keep ordered and clean, to hang in wardrobes in familiar groupings. Or that she hated them; looked at them hanging, empty, while his body was off betraying elsewhere. Or maybe held them, with memories I didn't like to imagine, remembering passion, once. Or maybe not that at all; perhaps just indifference, gentle indifference. Wanting, simply, to know what was what, and looking elsewhere for her peace and consolation.

I wonder if Isobel and I would have liked each other. Loving the same man; probably for different reasons. If she did still love him. She must have loved him once. Wondering, for her, what wore it down; what ceased to be attractive and became irritating. When the accustomed, the familiar, became dull. Joylessness seeping in. Somehow expecting it to have been different from Bill and me; who had begun with so few words, so very little to dry up. Thinking, as my mother would probably have thought, that surely they had known better, or understood differently. Their lives were not measured in pay packets, pools money, co-op dividends, rent; as if there was purer air above all that which might make decisions cleaner and clearer. And realising that that was probably not true. That it was probably no different at all.

Only once Robert and I spent a night away together. We went to Devon on a clear day in April. In all our four years together it was the only occasion when we rewrote our own stories, that night, that one night, when we shared a bed. Lying there, imagining how it might have been. The next day we walked on the beach, scrunching the shingle beneath our feet, and watched the gulls wheel high overhead, calling and squabbling and slicing down into the grey water with a flurry and folding of wings. Robert painted me sitting on a rock, some pebbles in my outstretched hand. Sitting there, the salt taste on my lips, my skin tingling from the wind, the cold of the rock on my hip, milk-water sunshine coming from behind the clouds, warming my fingertips and catching the flint-edge of the stones.

Martha the mermaid, Robert laughed, *luring men to their fate, or at least me to mine. I think I shall give you a tail*, he said, *a blue and pink iridescent tail.*

Fine, I replied, *just don't ask me to sing.*

Sitting there, my shoes turned to flukes. Later, by the water's edge holding Robert's hand; remembering how it had felt that morning to open my eyes and see his face on the pillow beside mine. The sea at my feet swelling blue and grey. The pebbles from the painting still in my pocket. Clutching them, squeezing them, making them mark my palm. Witness to the moment, to that perfect joy.

Everything has to end, has to somehow stop. I know that now, and I knew it then, but knowing something isn't the same as accepting it. Accepting means swallowing the unpalatable like a cold, hard pill. Living with endings is the hardest part. It's only recollecting this, sitting here in my chair, that the irony of being on a bus strikes me now. Did I measure out my life in bus rides, I wonder? Shopping, visiting, fetching, carrying; sitting on buses with my chattels on my lap. So it's not a coincidence, not unlikely, that so much of what happened with Robert I remember in relation to being on a bus. Perhaps that's my epitaph: Martha, who loved Robert and rode on buses.

That day, sitting behind two women, one of them wearing a headscarf with a gauzy pattern, the scarf knotted tightly beneath her chin, as if to clamp her jaw or stop something escaping. The other woman with the local paper on her lap, reading out the choice bits to her jaw-locked friend. Like two old crows, pecking at a flattened rabbit on a road. Then her saying, *can you imagine it, Robert Lawrence, he used to be my sister's doctor. Collapsing and dying in the surgery it says. Massive heart attack. What a way to go. Surgery full I imagine.* Peck peck peck.

136

And me leaning forward, over the silver handrail, the newspaper print fuzzing and blurring and resuming its shape. Robert Lawrence, died, died, dead. Rearing up in my seat. Needing to get off the bus; *excuse me please*, to the woman next to me, *I have to get off*. Barging past, bags in my hand, hanks of dread in my throat. Lifting my hand to press the bell, just beyond a stop but pressing it anyway, and as I lifted my hand the carrier bag breaking, shopping spilling out. A cabbage bump bump bumping down the aisle after me, a milk carton catching my ankle, laddering my tights. The bus conductor saying *Mrs . . . Mrs . . . your shopping*. But not stopping, just getting off and running, pitiable and jerky, stumbling in my shoes, but not stopping.

Running back to our first churchyard, from that day in May. Running to a saddle-back roof, a bench and a lilac tree. The sobbing starting; huge wrenching sobs rising like shapes in my throat, blocking my wind-pipe until my head was dizzy with grief. Reaching the church and falling on my knees next to the wall; my forehead pressed to the stone, my knees on the flagstone path. Weeping and crying and banging my palms on the wall, and saying his name over and over, as if by will I could make him appear. Conjure him to walk up the path and wrap me in warmth, in the wool of his jacket, the smell of his skin. Instead, the crusty lichen pressing onto my cheek, the damp sourness of the stone. Alone, on my knees, in the gathering shadows.

Kneeling there, for hours. The twilight wrapping me to the stone, crying until I was heart-sick. And the worst part, the unbearable part, imagining it all. Thinking of him in his surgery, whether he was alone or with a patient, or walking to the waiting room, or writing a prescription. How much pain, how much knowledge, how much time. What he thought. How much indignity, how much intervention. And the searing realisation that all that detail would be Isobel's; that his last moments would be pieced together for her. That she could see him, sit with him, see the life gone out of him, while I could not.

In the half-light, an awkward young curate coming to lock up the church. Looking at me quickly, probably sniffing for alcohol, the shopping around me, the split bag completely open. Assessing whether I was a tramp, a bag-lady, or a deranged parishioner. And wanting to say to him, as he hesitated by the door, that this was how it was. Not Jesus in a blue cloak reaching out his hand to cherub faced children; suffering them to come unto him whilst clean, smelling of vanilla, with milk-teeth smiles. Instead, a fat old woman, splayed out in a churchyard, a pack of sausages around her, and cracked eggs, and a quarter of lard with the corner all squashed, on her knees with grief. The curate stepping forward and asking if he could help, offering to fetch the vicar and asking if I'd had a turn or a fall, or if there was something I would like to talk about. And replying no, no, please no, thank you. Stumbling and shambling to my feet. Stuffing sausages into the other bag, using the egg box to scoop up the broken shells. Tidying up. And the curate walking away, thinking I was perhaps better left to God. Perhaps preferring grief of the hand-patting sofa-sitting kind. Not this mess.

Walking home, nursing my impossible, solitary, secret grief. Feeling sliced in two not only with loss, with longing, with disbelief, but also the knowledge that I could say nothing, tell nothing, show nothing. The realisation that for the rest of my life I would be alone because not with him.

The ridiculous thing, I kept thinking of Isobel too; of what she might be thinking and feeling. Whether she was lying awake, or had been given something to help her sleep, or whether she was sitting surrounded by all her mountains of his things. Mourning her husband, all those years of patterns and habits and memories and homes; of rooms with first one wallpaper and then another. Old black and white polaroids; Kate, tiny, sitting on their laps. What he had been to her, what he may have become to her, how she saw it all. Perhaps she was furious; mourning her unfaithful husband, teeth gritted, because he never came clean.

Her husband, my lover. Acknowledging all the ties and claims she had to him, the rightfulness of what they shared. Night after night, when one has a cough and keeps the other awake, talking quietly in the early hours. Isobel making fine lunches and complicated sauces, pounding herbs from the garden in her pestle and mortar, and calling him into lunch. Yet I had my claim too. Spines laced together in a churchyard in July. Wishing I was dead too and could be buried with him; that all the layers would fall away and our bones powder together.

Grieving because I had no things, no photographs, none of his clothes, nothing to hold. Nothing to take in my hands and press to me. When he was alive it had not occurred to me. Now in death, as if he had vanished. That first night, lying in my bed, pole-axed. Even now, unspeakable.

On the day of the funeral I sat in his village churchyard on a small bench, dressed in my ordinary clothes and holding my book, so that if anyone looked twice I would seem to have a purpose.

It was a bleak, grey, October day. Most of the leaves had fallen from the trees and were huddled in wet heaps up against the wall. There was a fine drizzle in the wind, the kind that seems not to touch you but then soaks you through. The congregation arriving; noticing, despite myself, how well-turned out they were. Wellshod women, with fine scarves at their necks and leather gloves that went up past their wrists. Recognising Isobel, pale and stiff, taking refuge under a hat. The coffin with late roses on top, carried slowly up the path. Through the lych gate and close enough that I could have reached out and touched it. Sitting stone-still, my nails in my palms, the crazed-grief madness making me want to run to him, open it, hold him and wail. But not moving; knowing and respecting that all this was Isobel's, yet not being able to stop scalding, scalding tears as the hymns drifted out through the door. That moment, that day, that bleak empty sense of loss, never to leave me.

Watching the coffin carried out on the west side. The soil banked high, and brown and fresh. The rain leaden and spiteful now. Weeping at the thought of him in all that wormy damp and cold. Realising that so much of how I saw him (the colour of his eyes, the blue spring sky I first met him under) was full of light, of delphinium blue light, so that I could not bear the thought of him in the dark, pressed in. Even though I tried to tell myself it was just his body; that what had been him, was him, was not in there, I could not bear it. And, in a ruffle of pettiness, bridled too that he was not to be placed in the south side, knowing how he loved a good rose window.

Watching Isobel and Kate throw earth on the top, not near enough to hear the sound of it on the wood. Isobel paler still, yet seeing her wrapped in the consolation of other people's words. And yet I was not hungry for their words, I was hungry only for him. I wanted to close my eyes and open them at a stranger's funeral. For Robert to be sitting at my side waiting for the service to finish so that we could go into the church and see a chancel arch or a three decker pulpit, or an alternating row of

Norman and Perpendicular clerestory windows. To be sitting on the bench talking quietly with him, his arm around the small of my back, nothing an inscription on a tombstone of a long-dead child, who wrote on slates and wore serge pinafores. That was what I wanted to be seeing, not this, not Robert's final church.

I watched until the gravediggers had replaced all the soil, until Robert was under a mound of earth, with all the flowers and wreaths laid on top. I had no flowers, no words to bring. Instead, I knelt down, stiff-kneed, cold-legged, and took out my book, my *Guide to English Parish Churches*, and pushed it into the soil to turn to dust with him. It was all I had, you see, it was all I could give. Each page a memory of time spent with him, Robert and I turning to each other in sunlight, in November greyness, laughing, talking about something. Belonging.

In tears again, flowing into my lap. Saying softly, *my love, my love* to a mound of earth. Knowing then, as I know now, that the rest of my life would be spent replaying him back.

Afterwards, the pattern of my life with Bill not really changing. The coal fire stoked a little higher on autumn evenings. Both feeling the damp more, the chill more, the cold creeping in. Endless conversations with Robert in my dreams. His body before me, alive and warm, tumbling together in a fudge of memory and desire.

Sometimes, nightmares when I lost him, where he walked between tombstones calling to show me something and I could not follow. Or catching the wrong bus, or stepping into the wrong car, running to meet him and always in the wrong place. My dreams peppered with the flotsam of everyday life. Often, things in my hands, my iron or Bill's boots, and once a pestle and mortar that I knew was not mine, but which I had to return.

Understanding my life was not a sequence of events, instead, all of it transparent, folded on top of itself. Nothing goes away, even if you want it to. Realising too that I had no words that could really tell it as it was. That I only knew what it felt like that first day, and that all I could do was to let myself love. To have not loved Robert would have been to sleepwalk through my life. Harbouring a stubborn view that God might see the rightness of it, in the midst of all that was wrong. Long ago prayers and psalms. Lord have mercy on us. Christ have mercy on us. Let my cry come unto thee. And it occurred to me that maybe losing him was my punishment. That secret, aching, agonising grief my payment to God. That I have grown older still, my body cracking around me like an old chrysalis, whilst paying my dues. Old feet in old shoes, with slipper satin memories.

And with what was left of my heart being kind and considerate to Bill. Coming home to find him always in his chair by the fire; the skin of his cheeks furrowing down onto his collar; his hands resting on his middle and snoring softly. A suck-in of air and a whistle of it out; the new rhythm of his day. First diabetes, and then his kidneys, until he went into hospital with a small brown suitcase filled with pyjamas and a puzzle book. Sitting on the bed while I packed it all, like a child sent to school. Him saying, hesitantly, *Not much to show is it?* His life boiled down to three sets of pyjamas, a blue towel, slippers, a dressing gown and a puzzle book. Wondering what it was he wanted me to say. If that's what he was seeking. Words that would make it better or easier or different. Or just less alone. Wondering why he might choose words now; falling from his mouth like white pebbles, heavy on his lips. Falling on the bed between us, while I folded pyjamas and smoothed down the crease with the side of my hand. Sensing his anxiety and knowing there was nothing I could do but continue to fold; to loop the dressing gown tie round and round in a whorl of towelling. Standing by the bed, clicking the suitcase shut, and seeing through the net curtain out onto the street and watching a child on a bike going up and down the kerbstone, weaving and bumping and jolting, a spatter of dried mud up the back of his coat from riding in puddles. And Bill so still, and the child in the corner of my eye always moving, and the net curtain stirring in the slightly open window. And me doing nothing to disturb it all. Putting the case on the floor and smoothing out the bedspread; noticing that he never took his eyes away from my hands. Wondering if he always saw fabric in my hands like I saw washers in his. Wondering but not asking. Knowing that it would be an intrusion, and better to keep smoothing and ordering. Silently. While he walked, heavy-footed, glancing at the window, from the room.

All the time I knew that it was some form of goodbye. Not the final one, but the one in our bedroom. The room of all those years of starting and ending days, of shuffling in and out of clothes, of lying, sleeping, side by side. The window open in the summer, the extra blanket on from October. Familiarity and separateness, all at once. And thinking again of what Robert and I would have made of such a chance. The chance to say goodbye in a blizzard of words and tangled limbs. Knowing that I would have held him and held him and held him, blind to the child, to the curtain, to the rumpled bedspread. Only wanting that he should never fear, never hurt, never be pained. That I would be with him, in him. Always.

Then, shaking myself back, looking to see if there was anything else of Bill's I could add to the case; anything to make his cubicle on the ward more familiar. Thinking, not unkindly, how most of his life had been marked by an absence of conversation and an absence of things. That what captured him most were his plumbing bag, his fishing bag, his darts set, and the old broken bucket from the pigs. Then, going downstairs and finding him out in the yard, leaning on the rain barrel, looking at

145

the border, the straggled brown remains of plants, the stones flint-edged in the bare soil, a flock of starlings wheeling high in the sky, and yesterday's rain still puddled and pooled in the tin roof of the pig sty, and his boot pressing on a fat strip of moss between the paving. Bill still saying nothing; taking the case from my hand and walking down the path. Noticing, as I walked behind him, the stoop of his shoulders, the bone-aching weariness of his walk. Choked by sympathy, beginning to reminisce about the pigs. Filling the cold February air that smoked from my mouth with pink gingery pigs and September sunshine and slices of light and the smell of apples, and huge rear ends shifting against the back of the sty, and Bill shovelling and mucking out with sleeves rolled up and his cap pushed back. And both of us smiling as we walked past the boy on the bike. United in the memory of snouts and trotters.

Coming to visit him each day on the ward. Sitting by him all afternoon while the doctors tested and checked and sampled. Wires in and tubes out. Plumbing him up. Sitting by the bed and looking at his hands all still and obedient on the overturn of the sheets. His hands looking so big and weak and clean; his fingers sometimes tracing the edge of the sheet. Watching him sleep, placing my hand on his hand. Remembering his young hands, twisting the washer, long ago, in Mrs Trewitt's shop. His young strong hands somewhere inside the heavy ones on the sheet. Somewhere in there, under all that sediment, from long ago. And thinking of all the things that hands could do. All the buildings built, all the books written, all the instruments played, all the new things made and invented. And his hands none the lesser for it. His hands that had done their bit. Quiet and true.

Wondering what secrets he had from me. If any. And what he had thought I had done for those four years. If he had guessed anything, known anything, regretted anything. The truth not heavy in my mouth. No wish to tell. No death bed confessions to trouble him on his way. Just wondering. Just wondering what he had thought.

One morning in March, Bill dying quietly; dying quietly in his sleep with no fuss. As if leaving the room to fetch something; unannounced and with no trouble. When I reached the hospital to visit him, the nurse was waiting by the ward entrance. *Mrs Fraser, I must talk to you.* Shepherding me into a side room, her face all tight with awkwardness. Probably wondering what I would do, how I would react; probably not relishing the prospect of a sobbing old woman with the ward so busy and so many to see to. Telling me that she had tried to telephone to let me know; that the phone had rung and rung and rung while I was out buying fruit to bring to him. Listening to her talking, and all the time seeing the phone ringing on the little table in the front room; ringing and ringing to the silence. Wondering if I had failed him in that too; whatever comfort it may have brought him to have me sitting beside him I was not there. Concentrating again on what she was telling me; that he had been asleep, that it had happened very quickly; his heart seizing and stopping while his kidneys pumped on.

Not crying. Not crying at all. Just sitting and listening and taking it all in. A widow now, but with the secret widowhood still so raw, still such a wound, that crying would be for both and so not fair. Walking, instead, to his bedside, the curtain pulled all round. The tubes taken out and wiped and cleaned and put away. Neatly probably. Someone else's rosary. His eyes closed and his hands over-lapping on his chest. Leaning over and kissing them, with tears in my eyes. Knowing I would mourn him, not with the anguish and cracking that I felt for Robert, but with affection and gratitude and know-ledge. The familiarity of a road long travelled together. In the knowledge that the way is hard, the wind can cut through you, and shoes chafe. Sitting there, next to my dead husband. My husband of the every-day: of the blue Formica table, of the stitched feather eiderdown, of Manny Solomon's brick-red chairs. My husband of decades com-menting that spring was a long time coming. Of trying to make the coloured lights on the Christmas tree work, endlessly rotating and twisting the pointed little bulbs.

Years of knowing the little things. That he didn't like mince pies. Or trifle. What toothpaste he preferred. That woollen jumpers fridged his skin, unless over a good thick brushed cotton shirt. That on a cold January night, with a cough on his chest, he would ask for Vicks vapour rub and smell of eucalyptus and mint. And the look of his writing on the boys' birthday cards, and on old plumbing bills. As if his hand had never quite got accustomed to the feel of holding a pen. Surprised by ink.

The nurse again, bringing me forms to sign, before I left the hospital. Stepping outside and walking back to the bus stop, the wind slicing through me and the daffodils jarring against the grey squalling sky. The yellow, and the grey, and the black spikiness of the bare trees. The branches rattling against the roof of the bus shelter. A crow blown backwards, cawing with rage. Buttoning up my coat, a quiet calm inside. Mourning Bill, but accepting his death. Not knocked to my knees as for Robert. None of that anguish, that howling, that grief. Just gratitude, affection, and relief that it had been peaceful. Comfort in the thought that I could take care of him at his end, sort out his things, make sure it was the way he would choose. Do it with kindness, not the resignation of a stranger, picking up clothes in finger and thumb, stuffing envelopes with a watch or a photograph. As it will be for me.

At his funeral, a few of his friends from The Crown, and some from the Council plumbing works. A woman from The Crown too, who organised the darts fixtures. Looking a bit like me, but not; the make-up heavier, the mouth harder. The shoes a little higher, the strap cutting into her ankle. Looking me up and down, her eye a bit judgemental. Saying he was a good man, but tartly, as if I might not know. *To think, all those years*, she said, *and we never saw you down there*. Me never having considered it an option. *He always said you were busy with your own things. Busy busy*. Her eye flickering slightly. Me wondering, fleetingly, if she had ever stepped in. Wondering if she was standing talking to me with knowledge strapped to her like a breastplate, and not minding if that was the case; that she made my betrayal easier. But also knowing he probably hadn't; that Bill would live by the rules, unlike Robert and I who justified making our own.

And now, aged eighty-two, all of this long enough ago and yet still with me. Always with me. Living in my own home until two years ago, when suddenly I couldn't be bothered any more. Choosing this nursing home with its big bay windows so that I could look out and see. If everything crumbled, if my limbs or my mind failed, I could just sit and look out, be sucked into the available light. That not happening yet; instead, playing whist and dominoes and still reading books. Still finding new words and holding them precious in my mouth. Listening to the school children coming in to sing carols or to play their recorders. A hairdresser coming on Thursdays. Not minding the routines; the coffee at eleven wheeled in on a trolley, the warm milk settling to a thin skin on the top. The cooking better than mine. Still able to iron my own clothes; not relinquishing that yet. The vicar of St Agatha's coming each Thursday to visit. Patting our hands and making small talk. Smelling, in my mind, of uncooked sausage and egg.

All that until today, and now my room filled with Robert. Here on my bed, everything restored. Things that are familiar, things I have never seen. Some kind of blessing, from Isobel, to give these things to me after so many years.

Our *Guides to English Parish Churches*; mine not seen since that day by the graveside when I pushed it into the bitter, dark soil. Inside the first page, *To Martha, Love Robert*, the ink soft and faded from that churchyard in May. And the paintings, none of which I had ever seen, only the first sketches, on those days, in those places. I am resplendent, silver and pink, sprinkled with blue petals and with jewels in my hands. I, a plain woman, thick ankled, broad-beamed, am a mermaid on a beach, with rubies in my outstretched hand, my iron a sceptre glinting on the shoreline.

All of it back before me, forcing sweet tears. His diary telling me how much I was loved. Hearing again the sound of his voice. That night, at his death, with nothing to hold. Now, all these years later, my lap overflows.

To Isobel, I feel gratitude that she should have done this thing. Chosen, freely, to give all of this to me. In that, surely, some kind of peace. Not done in anger, but in some kind of faith. Faith perhaps that I loved him, loved him with conviction. That in reality, my life amounts to little else.

I will choose to be buried with these things; I will hold them to me, my bones to dust. I have no-one to leave them to; no-one to tell. No-one for whom they would not cause pain. And when I am dead, whichever nurse sorts my things, she will find the instructions, what I wish to be done. I am sure she will look, just one quick look, and see me naked, delphinium-blue, arms outstretched, in a field in June. She will probably think, perhaps unbelieving, how surprising this is. Will talk to the other nurses at the shift changeover time; *Whoever would have thought it, Martha Fraser indeed?*

Martha Fraser indeed. In word and in deed and in thought and in body. All that I can say, all I can know that I did, was to love him and be loved. To be full of it; pulsing with it. Jam-packed with love.

And that's all I said, when Sheila the night nurse came in. *This was my beginning,* I told her, *jam-packed with love.*

CHAPTER 5

SHEILA

A remedy against sin

Brazen I suppose some might call it. It's certainly not what you expect to see, going about the rooms before bedtime, just checking that the able-bodied ones are in their nighties and pyjamas, no hot drinks by the bed which might spill and burn when they reach to turn off the reading lamp, everyone toileted nicely, the infirm ones bedwashed and tucked up. A careful eye swept over the room, that's how I like to think of it; not done in an intrusive or overly-bossy way. Just competence, lightly disguised; a few words, a warm smile, all the time making sure everything's as it should be.

I'm fond of my last-minute night check; thorough and kindly, that's what I aim for. And so, when you're looking for cocoa, perilously placed, or a lamp wire trailing where it might cause a fall in the night, it's a bit of a surprise to see paintings, nude ones at that, oil on canvas spelling out desire and knowledge in a way that is instantly recognisable; nudity in a style that I can only describe as non-medical. I'm not a prude, at least I don't think I am. I can't claim to be overly familiar with that aspect of life, but I wouldn't describe myself as prudish.

Years ago, when I used to work in the maternity hospital, that was different. In a funny way, sex was in the air then, all the time if you think about it, or there wouldn't have been all those pregnant women, would there? And it was all so clear; all those women's bodies, so blood-packed and pulsing, all that pushing and twisting. You recognised, even if you were just changing the bed sheets, that it was all about sex and life and blood and redness. Pictures like those ones perhaps wouldn't have even caught your eye, not in that environment.

But here it's all different; geriatric nursing couldn't be more different. It's as if everything has been bleached out, to emphasise that all possibility of the other has fallen away. Every day, I look at lips that have faded to the colour of old tea roses; eyes that have become a watery blue, white-rimmed like egg yolk. Veins, like washed-out ink, that snake along the backs of hands. I brush hair that has dimmed to grey or white; I wash underarms that retain only a few straggles of hair. I pat dry skin that is no longer pink, but parchment. And it's hard to imagine these bleached out bodies, these men and women – even the ones who can still have a little joke, or tell me a well-worn story that comes out from their lips

154

creased through repetition – even these ones it would be hard to imagine like in those paintings. I work with fading, that is how I think about it; a fading of all things physical and mental, and then of life itself. And those paintings, they weren't about fading at all. Even I could see that.

Which is why, I suppose, seeing all Martha's things gave me such a jolt. Not just the reminder that all the people here were so different once, but, I have to admit, the age she is (for it is clearly her) in the paintings. She looks about sixty, five years younger than me. That's the thing that has started me thinking. Usually, I just sit here thinking this and that, waiting for a red light to wink from the panel to call me to someone's bedside, or waiting for the little bell to ring as a reminder to go and turn over the ones who have had strokes so that they don't get bedsores. Yes, usually, all is calm and peaceful in my little night office. I sit at the desk (some of the others sit in the armchair, but I never do; that way lies the drift into a nap, and the unseen light or the unheard bell, and in the morning something that is undeniably your fault, a small, unmeant neglect while you dozed in the Parker Knoll). No, I sit at the desk, often with a nice cup of tea; sometimes my knitting, occasionally a small puzzle or a cross-word. Experience has taught me it's important to keep the brain lightly ticking when you're on night shift; and then you can think properly if you have to (like when Mrs Walker fell and broke her hip and I had her off to A&E within fifteen minutes of hearing her cry out).

And now, I find myself here thinking of Martha. Surprise really, layers and layers of surprise the more I think about it. Firstly because she never says much anyway, let alone anything of a confiding nature, and yet there she was, looking at herself as a mermaid as if she was breathing in each daub of the paint, her broad old legs turned to a glittering tail. She looked as if perhaps she'd never seen it before, or as if somehow it had taken her back either to that day, to where it was painted, or, most probably to who had painted it, I should think. Sitting there on the bedspread, she looked as if she could taste the tang of a salt wind off the water, and her skin glowing from it all. At the same time as taking her in, I was looking at the picture, and wondering why there was an iron painted amongst the pebbles, an iron all silvered and beautiful so it was like a sceptre rather than something to press out creases. It had love writ large all over it, I could sense that, even though I would not describe myself as someone with an eye for art. And knowledge, too, it had knowledge there. Sometimes, I've watched those programmes on television when they spend ten minutes explaining a painting to you – there's always much more to it than I could ever imagine – and they say about whether the painter knew the woman, or if she was a sitter, or perhaps a daughter. Well, I could never write a television programme about a painting, but I do know this. That painter knew her, knew her in a way that doesn't make me think they had been married forty years and were used to watching each other pull on their shoes of a morning.

Martha's words, what she said to me, *This was my beginning, jam-packed with love*. The certainty with which she said it, as if everything before had faded into insignificance. Imagine, the thought of starting it all then, now, at my age, when I've ruled it out for years. If I think of myself, of my marriage with Henry, of what we do, of what I like to do, it seems unthinkable, impossible even, to be sprinkled with delphiniums on old breasts, or to be painted holding a bowl of plump gleaming cherries like someone from a Greek myth. At this age, when I like best to sit with a cup of tea in front of the television watching *Coronation Street*, or a walk in the park with a nice bag of sherbet lemons, handing one to Henry and watching him carefully twist the wrapper into a ball before putting it into his pocket. And in June, perhaps going on a day trip to Brownsea Island, catching the ferry from Poole, a basket of sandwiches on my lap, tomatoes sliced neatly with ham and mayonnaise, all wrapped tightly in foil with nice crimped edges. I don't think of this as my endings – I'm not saying that – but they are not my beginnings, not in the way that I think Martha meant. They are, I think, my conclusions, they are the destination Henry and I have reached together.

My beginnings, I think, were altogether different. There has only ever been Henry really. I kissed one man before him; I remember the impression of stubble, of sour whisky, and a thick bottom lip. In retrospect, I can see that this fleeting impression worked well in Henry's favour.

I first met him in a park, on my lunch hour when I was training to be a nurse. He worked in an office nearby, and used to sit on a bench by the pond and eat his sandwiches while watching the ducks. I would be sitting on another bench, usually with Rosemary, my friend, usually laughing about some old consultant at the hospital, or some strict old matron, and I would notice him, sitting quietly, sometimes reading a paper, his sandwiches always wrapped in thick waxed paper.

What I noticed first was how clean he seemed to be; his nice gabardine raincoat, his hair always neatly combed back. When I walked past I noticed how clean his fingernails were, how carefully he folded up all his lunch packaging and put it in the bin. The first day he spoke to me was when Rosemary was off with a cold. He was so polite; asked me if I would like to go for a walk around the pond, and we talked about the ducks, and about how the leaves were turning early this year.

He told me he lived with his mother, that his father had died young, and a week later, invited me to Sunday lunch, telling me not to worry, just to bring myself. His mother opened the door and looked me up and down in a way that took me all in. Not that there was much to object to, I have to say. I would describe myself, then, as halfway pretty; always nicely turned out, and very particular about the feet. My shoes are always more expensive than I can really afford. She greeted me quite formally, and asked me inside, and I was struck straight away by the dimness of the light, the thickness of the net curtains, the spider plants in pots which seemed to have tinged the room green with their thin, striped leaves.

In the kitchen, Henry smiled his greeting and carried on laying the table. I noticed how carefully he lined up the knives and forks, touching the end of each one with the base of his thumb to make sure they were correctly spaced to the edge of the tablecloth. I remember asking his mother if I could do anything to help; she replied that doing the gravy would be a good idea. *Making a good gravy stands you in as good a stead as anything*, she said, which possibly has more wisdom in it than I credited her with at the time.

I stood there, mashing the onions from beneath the beef into the gravy, pouring over the potato water, and stirring it carefully with a wooden spoon. After lunch, we went for a walk, and when I left to go home, he kissed me on the cheek. How respectful, said Rosemary, when I told her the next day. With hindsight, I don't think she knew as much as she thought.

Henry asked me to marry him about two months later, on the same park bench, on a cold day in

159

November, and all I could think, when he asked me, was how decent he was, how clean and how shy. How much of a contrast to my rip-roaring father, who came home of a weekend night smelling of beer and piss, so that my mother told me *whatever you do, do not marry a man with an eye for the drink*. Perhaps, in retrospect, that was what I thought then; that whomever I was marrying it was certainly not a man with an eye for the drink. Instead, it was a man with a clean gabardine coat, who smelt of soap and shoe polish and who liked knives and forks laid out just so.

I said yes, while the wind whipped round the bench, and while my fingers turned blue, clasped in my lap. I saw before me a neat, safe life; Henry with a scarf knotted properly at his throat when out on a cold February night; his mother's gravy recipe endlessly poured over Sunday roasts through the years. The toilet seat, I guessed, would never be left up.

On our wedding night, I didn't really know what to expect; although I knew enough to know that what happened wasn't what was meant to. That, put baldly, nothing actually did happen. When I think back, I can understand my uncertainty. At that time – it was the late 1950s – there were inklings of people living what we thought of as more modern lives – but certainly not us. No, we lay side by side under a sea-green candlewick bedspread and I lay there waiting, my hands palms down on my stomach, my face half turned to

Henry's in the dark, my tongue heavy in my mouth, thinking that perhaps he would know how to begin. I knew from nursing what the signs were; I was conscious of glancing down to the middle of the bed, looking for any indication that something might be imminent. But nothing. He turned to me, and held me, and kissed me with his lips together in a way that made it clear that nothing invasive was expected. I remember reaching out my hand to stroke his midriff above his pyjama waist, thinking perhaps that might let him know I would not be horrified by a turn of events in that direction, but I felt him turn his abdomen away, so clearly turn his abdomen away, that I put my hand back on the bedspread and continued to kiss him in a way that reminded me of two horses I'd seen nuzzling each other over a fence; a communion of sorts, but not what you'd hope for, lying there in your bridal nightie scrubbed clean as a fresh plum.

Each night, the same painful awkwardness, the same silence, the same *Goodnight dear* in a way that made it clear to me that he could now be released to go to sleep. I expect it's different now; I can't recall anyone asking Sarah if she was pregnant, or if she and Michael were hoping for a baby. I think people are so aware these days that couples might be having IVF, or that the woman might prefer working, that nobody really asks. It wasn't like that then; then, your newly-married status, six months in, was a licence to ask.

Standing in the greengrocer's queue, sprouts and potatoes in paper bags in your hand, and someone from the road you lived on asking you, *Any happy news yet?* or saying something about tiny feet, or looking at you sideways on with a skilful eye and a knowing look. And I stood there (always the memory of those moments smells of sprouts, and yet I hardly ever bought them) smiling, saying no, no with a small embarrassed laugh, and the tincture of those parch-dry bedtimes still on my skin in the morning.

One night, I remember Henry inadvertently coming into the bathroom while I was in the bath. I stood up, clumsily, quickly, in what I think was going to be an attempt to reach for the towel. I was having a period and as I stood up a plug of dark, glistening blood spilled out onto my thigh. His face, I remember so clearly, was appalled. His hand to his nose, as if trying not to scent me, his eyes horrified as if my entrails were slithering down my leg. And at the same pace as his horror, I could see his attempts to mask it; a clumsy reaching for the nail clippers, or whatever had brought him in there in the first place, a retreat out of the bathroom door that could not be described as unseemly in its haste. But I had seen him. I had seen what his face and his hand registered; I had seen in his eyes what my body, at that moment, was to him. The next day, I sat in the staff room with Rosemary drinking coffee, on the tip of my tongue the question I would not ask,

Does your husband ever look at you as if your body appalls him?

In February, after we'd been married a year and a half, I went to see Dr Hartley, our G.P. I sat in the waiting room, wondering how I'd find the words for it all; my shame at our soft, limp nights jostling with a desire to have a baby that had emerged, new and insistent, like a shoot. I sat in front of his desk, turning the edge of my cardigan sleeve in my hand, my words falling lamely onto the grain of the wood, *It's just that I'd like a baby, doctor, and nothing seems to be happening . . . each month I'm not pregnant.* And I presume, he'd asked, that there is no problem with intercourse? And there it was, the chance to spill it all out to him; to tell him of the nights of clamped-lip kisses, of a back turned firmly to me when I reached out to touch Henry. The opportunity to unfold it on the desk before him (morning glories, we called them on the ward, the possibility of telling him that we'd never even got as far as that), the difficulty of telling him all that and leaving Henry's dignity intact. Because each night it happened, each night as I lay there, my body frustrated, my skin raging to be touched, I was aware of the affection, the love, in Henry's voice as he said, *Goodnight dear*, sometimes his hand holding mine as he fell asleep. And I felt as if I was sitting in front of Dr Hartley with a lap full of hot shame; shame that was dripping around my ankles, staining the leather of my shoes. So I was not

163

surprised when I heard my voice say clearly, calmly, the lie coughed up from my throat like a smooth round marble, *No doctor, there's no problem with that, I'm wondering if there might be something just not quite right with one of us.* Give it another six months, he told me, and then come back and we'll talk again.

I've got a photograph that was taken of me around that time; in a studio, properly. I think it was a birthday present from Henry to me. I'm wearing a lemon dress – which still strikes me as an odd colour to have chosen. The picture's black and white, it doesn't show the colour of course, but I found the photograph recently, and remembered the colour instantly. I look like a big boiled sweet, except without the sherbet inside. My hair is curled in a very neat roll. My hands are gathered into my lap and I'm looking off-left, in what I presume was reminiscent of the style of women I liked to watch in the cinema. Now, when I look at that young girl I think how neat she looks, how neat and small; not small in stature, but small in womanliness. No *femme fatale*, I think that's how you might say it. No buoyant bosom that carried with it the promise of fecundity and Arabian nights. I can see I look the sort of girl that a mother would be very glad to have her son bring home, because there would be no threat there, no alluring call to a bedroom full of clever moves and curling limbs and tilting pelvises. No, just a nice sensible girl with care-

164

fully done hair, wearing a lemon dress that is ill-conceived but well-intentioned. And what's more, a ready vessel for a gravy recipe. Now that I think about it, when you were born to older parents then, you were somehow catapulted straight into middle age when you reached sixteen. My parents dressed like the old people drawn in children's books, and my bosom seemed to emerge straight into a good sensible blouse. When I look at teenagers now, with jeans that hardly go above their groin, and bare, pierced navels, and skinny-cut t-shirts that are as if stuck to their ribs, I don't shake my head and think it's a disgrace, or that there's no mystery anymore, like my friend Mary Poole says. No, instead I think it was the mystery that got my generation into trouble in the first place, and the young today are better off without it and having their moment instead.

Six months later I went to Dr Hartley again, on a sunny morning in August. I sat before him, trying to banish a memory from a few weeks earlier, when, waking from sleep in the middle of the night, the air with the warmth it gets only one or two nights in June or July, and everything feeling so silken to the touch, my skin slightly sticky, and the windows open, and moonlight coming through the curtain, and I thought *It's now or never* and reached over, inside his pyjamas, and took him in my hand, hoping for a response, that he might just sweep me up and everything happen at last. Instead, he lay his hand gently on my wrist, taking my hand away, lifting it off as if I were a child in a shop ignoring a sign that said *Do not touch*, and his voice, almost painfully weary, that's how I still remember it sounding, saying to me *Sheila, love*, and then turning away, the silence like snowfall between us. And that's when I knew, all those years ago, that that part of our relationship would not change; that sex was not what he wanted from me. And I lay there – such a warm night it was, I swear I could smell the flowers from next door's garden, and such a lift in the air, such a sweetness and softness – and understood that in his voice, in the way he said *love*, that there was love, but not like the sort I'd been hoping for. Not the type that would have let me sit in front of Dr Hartley and say *Everything's fine, I think I'm pregnant*. No. I sat in front of him, the memory of that night like a cobweb on my skin, and told him I was certain there was a problem, what could he suggest.

To think, nowadays, of what a hurry-scurry of tests that would have induced; sperm counts and hormone levels and ovulation injections, and IVF, and clinics with walls and walls of photos of miracle babies. Women with tight jawlines and clenched hands and desperate eyes, coming for scans to see if their embryos had taken. Feeling like colanders, I expect, as if small molecules of life slipped through without trace. But back then, nothing of that. Dr Hartley hesitated briefly and then asked, *Have you considered adoption*, and I jumped at it, like you would a raft that could take you to the promised land.

I went home to Henry and suggested it, without any trace of embarrassment, any self-consciousness, with no allusion to the issue we never discussed. I thought he was going to throw back his head and roar with relief. It's funny, those moments in life when what is not said is more significant that what is; the knowledge, implicit between us, that what I was offering was a way off the hook for him. *What a wonderful idea*, he said. *What do we do?*

Birthing homes; what terrible places they were, stuffed full of teenage girls, stern matrons and correction. Whey-faced young women being punished for something most of them had not entirely understood. We waited in Reception and I watched them coming and going in the hallway; one with a belly neat and compact like a netball, walking up the stairs and tapping each of the spindles as she went, like a child going to bed. And another, with corkscrew curls and cheeks that were florid and rosy, like a drawing of a healthy country child, and who looked as if she should be out in the fresh air, birthing in the field and kicking up her heels with glee afterwards. It was such a sterile place – I remember being conscious of the irony of that – awash as it was with unplanned fertility, and with neat orderly queues of the infertile ready to take the babies away. The radiators and banisters and walls were painted a pale mint green. It matched the resolve, the moral certainty, in the staff's faces, as they went about their business, alternately chastising and bestowing, that's how it seemed to me.

When they brought the girl in, she was holding the baby so tightly I thought there might be a to-do about taking him from her. I was struck by how young she was – she can't have been more than sixteen or seventeen. She was shaking; her bottom lip was trembling, and I could see that she was biting into it with her teeth. I couldn't help but wonder where her own mother was; where she was while her child stood in front of us in a nightgown with bare feet, handing over her flesh and blood to perfect strangers. The brutality of it struck me then and still does now; although it was not enough, at the time, to walk away without the baby in my arms. It was a hunger, that's how I think of it, a gnawing hunger to have and hold a child that could be mine. I've often thought what a rag-bag of emotions those places held; all the wanting, the desire to possess, all those umbilical cords severed, some against the will.

Henry was sitting beside me, quietly taking his pen from his pocket, filling in forms and signing papers, and doing what the matron asked swiftly and competently. I couldn't look at the girl and I couldn't not look at her. I could see that she was sweating; damp rings marked the underarms of her nightgown, and one of her breasts was leaking

168

milk which made a patch across her front. I felt
dry, and small, and cruel, and as if somehow we
were nailing her feet to the floor. How respectable
we looked; Henry with his fountain pen, me with
my neat two-piece, and her sweaty and wet and
true in a way that pains me now if I think about
it, which, in truth I have not for years. Tonight,
and Martha, all of this tumbling through my mind
so that I cannot start my knitting or do the crossword, or even be bothered to go and make another
cup of tea.

She answered the questions matron asked her
as if someone else were operating her voice, and
all the time her arms were wrapped tightly around
the baby, her knuckles white, her veins visible.
Then, she handed the baby to the matron, and
matron wrapped him firmly and competently in
a white blanket and passed him to me. Like shopping, I thought, like being given a parcel after
waiting some time in a queue, and the girl turned
around slowly and walked out of the room.

When we left the building I was sure I could
hear weeping; I was sure that if I turned around
I would see her at an upstairs window. So instead,
I looked into my arms, at his small, puckered face,
at the small bead of milk still in the corner of his
mouth, at the curl of his dark hair on his scalp.
He's lovely, I whispered to Henry, and he smiled
and kissed me on the cheek and said, *I'm so glad
that you're happy*.

I called him Michael, and wrapped myself in a

baby cocoon, spun like a spider's nest with the three of us soft inside. I would place him between us in the bed, his tiny fingers curled around mine, the soles of his feet pushing against one of my hands. His arrival sprang us from the trap of our nights. Suddenly our sexless chastity seemed appropriate, somehow clean, in a bed that smelt of baby skin, of talcum powder, of clean terry nappies.

That first summer Henry dug over part of the yard and made a cutting garden. By July, it was a mass of flowers; delphiniums, larkspur, chrysanthemums, poppies. I would place Michael in his high chair and look out through the kitchen window and see them all, a swell of colour and movement and scent. I would carry Michael down in my arms and go along the rows, saying the colours, pointing to the birds, so happy I thought my heart would burst. It still amazes me how quickly I appropriated him and made him mine. I seemed to inhale the smell of his skin, the feel of him, absorb the weight of him into my ribcage until I couldn't contemplate that I hadn't birthed him. The girl with the horror-struck eyes faded from my mind, bleached away at the edges until she became indistinct.

I loved him; every minute of him. I was as clear about that then as I am now. He wasn't just a baby, a child; he tipped the balance of the scales and made everything right. I was able to love Henry, to enjoy Henry's company, without any of

170

the insistent nagging, the anxiety, the knowledge that all was not perhaps as it should have been. Michael was the guy rope that held it all up straight; the pulse that put the confidence back into my stride. I stood with him in my arms in the greengrocer's queue, asking for apples and carrots, letting old ladies thumb his cheeks, smiling when they said he was bonny.

I can still remember all the milestones so clearly; Michael wobbling on his shiny blue bike, Henry running alongside holding onto the saddle and me clapping and clapping on a cold frosty February morning saying, *You can do it, you can do it, you're doing it, you're pedalling by yourself*, and taking a photograph I still have, of him standing proudly beside his bike, his finger on the bell, wearing a navy duffle coat and a scarf I had knitted him.

Henry was just the kind of father I would have wished for a child. He was patient and kind, forever making little bits and bobs for him, out in the shed, the sound of hammers and nails, and afterwards some version of a suspension bridge held up with such pride by Michael that I would have kissed Henry on the spot if I thought that was what he would have wanted. On Fridays, he took him to the library, returning with books like *Swallows and Amazons* which he would sit and read to him in the armchair by the fire, and I would make hot chocolate and carry two mugs to them, and think of my own father and his boozy rages, and Friday nights that were torn with him banging on the door to be let in, and my mother hiding us in the pantry so as to be out of his way.

Friday nights always had, for me, the smell of beer, and anger, and the feel of the mop bucket crushed up by my foot, and the shelf with the flour and the sugar right up against my ear, and my mother moving quickly, darting like a bird, her voice cajoling, soothing, trying to jolly him upstairs, and beneath her tone, evidently, a thin note of fear, so when she closed the pantry door, her hand placed on the base of her throat, I could see a small pulse visible on the side of her neck, something tremulous about the way she swallowed. I would put the blanket over my sister and tell her to go back to sleep, and sit there until my knees had imprinted their shape on my chin, and wait for mum to come down and take us back up to bed, and in their bedroom the sound of my dad snoring fit to bust. So when I carried the hot chocolate in to my own front room, and saw Henry sitting and reading about boats out on lakes, and sandwiches cut for lunch, I could have dropped to my knees and given him thanks for it all. For the child, with the beautiful turn of his cheek and his eyelashes, sitting absorbed in the story, gazing as if he could see it all, and Henry from whom I had only ever seen kindness and goodness, and who somehow, healed all my Friday nights while reading to our child. And suddenly, we were in our thirties, with Michael at the grammar school, buying dictionaries for Latin homework, and geometry equipment in gold and blue tins, and moving house to one where we could park the car in the front driveway.

And it occurred to me, one lunchtime when I had just returned from a morning shift at the hospital, as I was unpacking some shopping and beginning to make shepherd's pie for tea, that here I was, thirty-seven in the spring, and still a virgin, still with no knowledge of sex and how it might be.

Just once, there was one of the hospital porters, a huge man who could take the trolleys with just one of his hands and used to wheel them along whistling softly to himself. As I was arranging the pillows for a patient he was fetching from theatre, he looked at me in a way that was ripe with possibility, a twinkle in his eye that was an invitation to smile back, and the other porter teased him and asked, *How come her trolleys are always delivered on the double?* and he laughed good-naturedly, and said, *Sheila's worth extra effort* and for a moment I wondered what it would be like to sleep next to him of a night. His hand on my breast, his leg resting across my belly. A light slap on my buttocks as I got out of bed. *Bring me some tea, love*, that was what he might say, sitting propped on the pillows, his chest all hairy, one huge hand behind his head. Toenail clippings, there would probably be those on the bathroom floor, realising, as he took the trolley from me, that perhaps my life matched Henry's more than I knew,

173

although that didn't stop me from blushing when his hand touched mine as I passed the trolley over.

For a while afterwards, when I saw him in the corridors, I quickened my step. I thought of my mother saying be careful what you wish for you might just get it, and knew what mattered most was my life safe with Henry and Michael. Sometimes, I watched a film at the cinema, and felt hot-skinned and sticky; a small pang of desire from watching the way the leading man kissed a woman, but it staying something to dream about, not something which made me look for it properly. Respectable my middle name. Henry and me, as if topped with some innocent 1950s pie crust; him with a slight crispness at the edges, and me bustier, my body slacker, my face peaceful, if slightly watchful, at all times. And my mother, not long before she died, sitting in her armchair and looking at me in a way she had which always conveyed more than she actually said, and saying, *Henry's such an old dear*, as if she had seen something that I hadn't, and it made me mindful of something she'd asked me years previously (*Sheila, dear, what is it that homosexuals actually do?*), and there it was, staring me in the face as I chopped onions for shepherd's pie on a white plastic board, that it was possibly that all along.

Then, two summers later we went on holiday abroad for the first time; went on an aeroplane to Spain, and sat in restaurants on the beach and ate paella and tried sangria, and Michael joined a group of other teenagers by the pool and Henry and I sat at the table and the waiter, who was what I would have then called flamboyant, swirled around us, putting our napkins into our laps, his fingers fluttery like butterflies, his smile white-toothed and his black hair oiled, and his walk, well, probably the word to describe it was mincing, but at the same time, a confidence, a comfort-ableness in his own skin. He moved around the table and took the order, and produced a saucer of olives with a flourish and I was mindful of Henry becoming agitated, annoyed, a small patch of pink visible at the corner of his mouth, and his fingers, unusually, clasped in a knot on the table. *How can he make such a fool of himself*, he said, when the waiter left, *prancing about like that for everyone to see. No self-control, no dignity. Ridiculous.* And I thought how unusual it was for him to comment on the behaviour of someone else, to be so nettled by a waiter taking an order, to appear so discomfited when the waiter returned to the table and lightly touched his shoulder as he placed his plate on the cloth.

Years later, when Michael was at university, we went to pick him and a friend up from the airport after they had spent the summer travelling in Europe. Michael sat next to me in the back, and was telling me about Rome and Florence and what he had seen there. In the front seat, Neil sat next to Henry who was driving, and whose face I could see in the rear view mirror. Neil fell asleep, his

175

head lain across his own shoulder, his blond hair bleached in the sun, his chest visible in his open shirt, and I saw Henry look across at him, once, just once, with a glance that struck me as furtive and ashamed, the corner of his mouth slightly moist, his lip tremulous, then a small pursing of his mouth, an almost imperceptible shake of his head. His glance was like a small, white hot flame, even I could see it as an expression of desire. A small surge, unwished for, and quickly harried away. And then I knew, sitting there in the back seat of the car, listening to our son talk about a cathedral in Italy, that for all these years it was not me, it was not personal. It was simply that I would never be able to provide him with what he desired.

A lavender marriage. I have learnt (reading in a magazine) that that is what it is called, when a man marries a woman as a smokescreen for his homosexuality. In retrospect, it seems unbelievable that I didn't piece it together sooner; my mother's observation, a waiter in a long-ago hotel, a drive from an airport when it was impossible to suppress. I wondered, at first, why someone chose lavender for the term. Was it for its fragrance which can cover and mask? Or perhaps for its medicinal properties, because it's supposed to soothe and calm. Why, I wondered, was it not called a rose marriage or a daisy marriage? But the more I thought of it (and I'm no psychologist, but I think sometimes if a word is to be applied to you, it's best to walk

176

around it, to consider it, to finger its edges like an old medal, until you can absorb it, accept it, and stick it to your chest) the more I realised the term is perfect. I mulled on lavender as I made beds, cooked meals, washed up, and learnt to see in it all kinds of relevance that help me understand things better. Lavender, you see, will flourish in the driest of soils, with the smallest amount of water. It will survive in the face of almost no nourishment. And it is clever in the difference between its appearance and reality – the sweet powerfulness of the fragrance is held up by its woody, dry stem. It is a plant without juices, without juiciness within, but which through drying and pressing produces a fragrance and effect that lasts. It helps people sleep, to lay their heads peacefully on their pillows at night. In sachets, it hangs from coat hangers and discourages moths. It preserves orderly housekeeping between folded sheets and linen, keeping everything pristine and freshly smooth.

I am almost sure that Henry has no secret life. I am confident that he does not visit toilets in lay-bys, or read magazines, or visit bars tucked away in side streets. I think he has buried this part of himself so deeply that now – when he is seventy-two – it may be of little importance to him. But I wonder, when he dreams, if that part of himself is free; or if he holds it like a sadness, or a small, howling rage. A wet, bundled towel, pressed to a bruise. One night, in bed, ten years ago now, I asked him through the darkness, *Do you think, Henry, you know, maybe, perhaps, other men?* And his voice dry and broken, as if fighting tears, *I never would. I never have. I am a married man. It is enough.* And I had a sense of what our lavender marriage meant for him; a mast he had nailed himself to, but which held him, on his terms, upright and correct; allowed him to look at himself in the mirror and see a married man staring back. And I reached over and held his hand, and kissed the side of his face, thinking of *Swallows and Amazons* and hot chocolate on long ago nights, and cutting beds full of flowers and a too kit that made trains and ferris wheels and suspension bridges, and I thought, as I think now, that there are different kinds of intimacy, and different ties that bind. And we have not spoken of it since; nor of the fact that our marriage has never been consummated. Everything I know has come from these small scraps, held unspoken, in my heart all these years, with our chaste nights like a canvas drawn tight over it all.

When Michael was so evidently heterosexual, I confess to a sigh of relief. It is easier, I thought, wanting his way always to be smooth. When he met Sarah I could see instantly that she was special, different; the way he looked at her, spoke of her, the way that she held his gaze. I asked him once if he had told her he was adopted. *I mentioned it*, he said, as if it carried no significance. I worried that she might consider me somehow less authentic, less valid, but it never seemed so.

Once, when I visited their flat early one morning, Sarah was still curled up in their bed, her dark hair flagged on the pillow, her knees curled to her chest. Michael made us some coffee and took some to her, and as he left the bedroom I saw him touch her face softly and reach down and kiss part of her ankle that was not covered by the duvet. It was done with such affection, with such pleasure in her substance, and when she came into the kitchen, her dressing gown knotted and wearing a pair of his socks, kissing me on the cheek and apologising for being such a sleepycat, she looked like a woman who knew that she was loved and desired, and I was glad for her, glad that my desiccated papery bed would never be hers. When she became pregnant, she became more fluid, more feline. I was proud of her; proud of the way she made it all look so easy.

I remember so clearly going to the hospital when Rory was born. As I came into the room I couldn't help but feel how lucky she was. Even though she was exhausted, and desperate for tea and toast, she was so evidently, so visibly consumed by the emotion she felt for her child, and it felt so proper and right, that a child should be welcomed so. I was unexpectedly sad, as I reached forward to hold the baby, wishing that moment had been mine, that Michael had been mine from his very beginnings. And yet so aware, as I kissed Rory's forehead, that this was another gift from Michael, another richness that would never have been mine.

We are both lucky, I thought as I handed Sarah back her child, and smiled at Henry, who was protesting that he could not hold something so perfectly tiny. It is not a question of blame, or fault, this has always been clear to me.

I had not thought of Michael's mother for years, yet by Sarah's bed I wondered again how it must have been for her, her body still leaking with traces of birthing as I took him away. When Sarah said, *I think we will call him Rory*, I wondered whether Michael had another name, a name that slipped away with no record or trace. As I stood by Sarah's bed, my hands became busy; professional, smoothing the corners of the sheets, making sure the corners were correctly tucked in. I felt both included and excluded, I can see that now, my hands distracting me away from a sudden desire to weep confused tears for us both. And yet, Michael's child felt so instantly my grandchild, and a warm step further away from my own beginnings as a mother. I remember fussing over Sarah, wanting to cocoon her and the baby, both for them and to banish the thought of the starkness of Michael's newborn time. (Again, at that moment, wondering where the girl's mother was; why she had not smoothed down bed corners and offered to spread butter on toast.) With each grandchild born, I have felt more solid, more involved; layers and layers of binding that hold us as a family.

I remember a song sung by that man with the big toothy grin who used to play the ukelele, the one about cleaning windows and all the things he saw within. I remember singing along to the radio, I can't have been more than fourteen, about two pairs of pyjamas side by side. I think of that, and the life Henry might have lived, and wonder if it hurts him, nowadays when there is no shame or notion of sin attached, to think that he has lived his life in a state of denial. And I have lived mine as a mother and as a wife and as a lavender shrub; firm to the ground, well-rooted, with a man who has been unfailingly kind and generous and supportive. In life, as we age, I think we learn, on our own terms, what is enough.

My marriage – and as I sit here at my night desk I can see it all so clearly, like a map of the stars, each one clear and distinct – my marriage consists of things I find utterly companionable, peaceful, and not without joy. We sit side by side at the breakfast table, and usually manage to complete the crossword. We like to try special-recipe sausages, served with mash and onion gravy. We make mulled wine at Christmas and go blackberry picking when the hedges are laden. We discuss what type of dog we would have, were we ever to have one. We sit on benches in the park, and watch our grandchildren play in the boating lake, and Henry reads to them, just as he did to Michael, and I make hot chocolate for them, and wonder how my hands got to be so old. We visit Michael and Sarah frequently for Sunday lunch, and Sarah laughs warmly and asks me to make

181

gravy like the children's great-grandmother. Henry builds champion constructions of Lego and Duplo, and he lies on the rug and the children clamber over him and I have a sense of mellowness, of fruition, of peace with it all.

Now, when I am sixty-five and Henry seventy-two, all of my anxiety, all of that hungry skin under a candlewick bedspread seems insignificant, almost unimaginable. In some ways, our chastity has left no real mark, nothing that I can turn to and say *this is the price I have paid*. My virginity is still upon me, if someone looked carefully enough, although I like to think I have the doughty demeanour of an old nun, when chaste innocence has been replaced by the wisdom of years.

I have never been desired. I know this and accept this. I have never lain in a man's arms and understood what it was all about. But I have held and loved my child, and I have loved and been married to a good man.

I wonder if Martha is sleeping now, and where she has put all her things? I wonder if she is holding them curled tight in her palm? I remember once as a child, I insisted on sleeping in new shoes, and railed at my mother in the morning when I found them neatly in the box beside my bed. I can still see Martha's portraits, the turn of her fish tail; her breasts covered in flower petals, her iron catching the light like a siren on the shore. I can see that her body is ringing with love, sex and boldness. *Jam-packed* she said, that was her term. It is not my word to use, but I will find my own. I do not feel insubstantial in the face of what I have seen tonight; sitting here, by my desk, I am not a desiccated heap of dust. I am solid and round and grounded like a fruit bowl. I can lie on the floor and feel the planet beneath me, layers and layers of it until it reaches hot rock. My marriage has been gently, quietly, chastely fraudulent, but also loving and kind and joyful and a provider of real companionship. I love Henry. I love Michael. I love Sarah. I love my grandchildren.

I feel as a bedrock, a foundation stone in all of their lives. I am loved in ways that are as valid as passion. I am happy, and can contemplate my past, and my future with serenity. This is what I know as I sit in my chair at my desk. I have my truth, just as Martha has hers.

CHAPTER 6

JUDITH

Bestow on this woman the gift of children

My evening course classes on Roman Civilization have engaged me in a way I had not anticipated. I was attracted to this class by the image of classical Rome. It is flawlessly white in my mind. Temples and columns with symmetrical grace, under an Italian blue sky, accessorised with togas that drape and fold like perfect ripples of wet sand. That is why I elected to take the course; I have long since given up feeling that things should be underpinned by worthy, rational thought. I started the course because of the white and the blue and the pleats; and the distant memory of Latin verbs conjugated with order and reason and matching endings, and I thought that here might lie some peaceful absorption.

The first week we began with the Greeks, which was something of a surprise. I had no thoughts about them and was without preconception. The tutor told us about Athens and Sparta, as part of a preamble on how we should not underestimate

184

the absoluteness upon which Roman civilisations were founded.

In Sparta, apparently, if a child was cold at night, they would cover it with a blanket of thistles and nettles. The plants would so irritate that the child would scratch and tear at its skin, until, presumably, it pricked red and warm with blood. So that's my image of the Spartans then; skin oozing warmth from a blanket of needles. He also said that if a woman gave birth to a child who was sickly or weak, they placed it out on the hillside to die. I prefer not to think about that, and was glad when he moved onto Rome.

The surprise of it all is how quickly the geometry of my preconceptions vanished. My, what a superstitious lot they were; how many rituals they wrapped around themselvs in this business of life. And this is what has so absorbed me now; not the blue and the white, and the cloth falling in folds, and the plaited leather of a sandal drawn in a book about Androcles and the lion I had as a child. No, instead, it is all the hocus-pocus; all the lesser gods and goddesses, with small, specific functions. All the rites and rituals, which, I presume, allowed the average Roman to leave the house in the morning and walk boldly forth to the market place or the forum and conduct themselves in a way that was calm and assured.

And I realise how many of the same preoccupations we share; how our world is both wholly different and instantly recognisable. A forum full of Romans trying to be safe, happy and make sense of it all is not so different I think from what preoccupies us still.

All that has gone before us, I realise, is out there somewhere. Layers and layers of the past that can be reached for as if through depths of water, and that somehow, in some way, rise up transparently clear. Time, I think, has a solidity of construct which is entirely of our making. I begin to think there is no ring-fenced past, no hermetically sealed future which both lie somewhere intact and perfect. Instead, it is all of an instant; all the same moments, accessorised differently. So I can see myself around a Celtic bonfire, wearing clothes made of hemp, my hair tangled. I can see myself on a Victorian *chaise longue*, a bottle of smelling salts in my hand, my neck ruffled in lace. I realise of course that this is probably part of my problem; that there is nothing solid, nothing I can hold onto and see as truly mine. A life imagined – I must not go there; instead I will think about doors and door hinges.

Last week, I learned about the goddess Cardea, who was also called Carna. She was the goddess of door hinges, and, by implication, of family life. She held in her hand a magical branch of flowering hawthorn, which could drive away evil spells from the openings of a house.

I am captivated by the idea of this; that with one swoosh she could banish anything from entering the house. I have looked at the hinges on my front door in a whole new way, and felt a taut respect

186

for their ease and power of facilitation. Short-lived, I'm afraid, because this week, we were taught about Forculus, a god who presided over the doors themselves, as distinct from the hinges. And, to complicate it further, we learnt about Portunus, a god who protected doors, but who became the protector of harbours as the word for door shifted in meaning. So where does that leave Cardea and her hawthorn branch? What autonomy did she have to decide if the door should or should not glide smoothly open? What if Forculus or Portunus thought everything would go swimmingly if a certain person entered the house, leaving Cardea to make the hinges fractiously turn, her hawthorn inept and twitching in her hand. What I don't understand is how all that can be regulated; *who gets to decide* is what I want to know. I would like to think that it was Cardea, but I begin to feel that it probably wasn't. I wonder if the appearance yet absence of power made her flick her hawthorn with frustrated spleen. My own door hinges have reverted to their previous invisible status. How many women, I wonder, think they have power or choice over something, and in reality realise they don't at all?

Childbirth, take that for example. The Romans had that covered. Twenty-four gods! Twenty-four deities, each with a specific responsibility for an aspect of birth. (I am wondering about mentioning this to my tutor – I have compiled a list – but I think he will interpret it as menopausal over-enthusiasm so best saved for private consideration.)

187

There were gods to be supplicated if a baby presented breech or head first. There was a god, Morta, of stillbirth, and a god, Sentinus, who bestowed consciousness before another god, Vagitanus, induced a newborn's first cry. There was a goddess to protect breastfeeding mothers, and one who looked after the child in the cradle, and one called Potina who presided over a child's first drink. There was Deverra, whose function was to protect babies from the evil tricks of Silvanus. At the time of birth, three people kept him at bay by sweeping the threshold with a broom, pounding the door with a pestle and striking the door with an axe. Edusa presided over a child's eating, and Stalinus over its first attempts to stand up.

All these gods, all this detail, focused on bringing a child from the womb to adulthood. I have little experience of children. From what I can gather, pregnancy consists of half a dozen visits to a G.P., an ultrasound scan, and a health visitor who comes to the house for ten days afterwards to check all is well.

I prefer, rather, the thought of women in child-birth being attended by midwives, with flowing hair and knot-free clothing. I like the thought of the pestle, the axe and the broom. I can feel their solidity and weight in my hand, and understand why they were chosen to stamp away evil. I like the idea of a god with the specific task of ensuring that a child's first drink is safeguarded; of a god who checks that the first hesitant attempts to stand result

188

in feet strong to the ground. I like this attention to detail; a different god for every position of a child in the womb, and for the distinction between the consciousness of the newborn and its very first cry.

What I also like is the feeling that, suppose a mother were not able to look after her child, there would be a host of deities on hand to ensure its safe passage, with relevant attention to all aspects of its life. So, if I picture a small boy sitting alone at a table, before him a meal, say, of pork chops, mashed potatoes, green beans and gravy, served on a cream chinaware plate with a Cornish blue rim. If, say, his mother was not there, to gently chide him to eat his vegetables, to finish his potatoes before putting on his hat and gloves and running out to the street (and understand I am not seeing a child, as he would be today, with wide-cut jeans hanging baggily on his hips, an over-sized t-shirt, a play station to hand. No, I am seeing a boy in a gabardine coat, with a home-knitted sweater, and a check flannelette shirt.) What I like is the thought that all that would be taken care of; that his steps to and from the house would be watched over by Adeona, that he would have eaten his meal because Edusa wanted him to.

What I am really saying is how cohesive it all seems. When I look, from an outside perspective, at how fractured it all looks today; at women at bus stops with children in pushchairs, the child drinking squash from a bottle, the women's faces tight, their mouths set against the cold, I think it would be comforting to have rituals and patterns wrapped around them like a soft, familiar sweater. To have names, and expectations, and rites of passage, which help them raise their child from newborn to adult. I don't think that ten visits from a health visitor probably counts as this; or a leaflet from the local library, pushed through the door, announcing the possibility of borrowing a new video outlining how to teach your child road-safety. (Pushing it through my door there was obviously no chance of an up-take, but it did make me think of what a small, gloved hand in mine might have felt like; probably how too infinitely precious ever to let cross a road alone.)

I am sensitive too, to what all the detail implies; to the danger inherent in the simplest mechanical action, like taking a drink, eating a mouthful of food, attempting to stand when there might be a risk of falling and dashing a head against a marble hearth. All these things, I know, point to how dangerous life could be; how necessary it was to be aware of peril at each turn. I know this, I don't need anyone to put me right on that one. All I am saying, I think, is that I like to think of a child kept safe. Safe from harm, from death, or whatever else might occur when you happened to glance in the opposite direction.

There was the same attention to detail when it came to the management of dying too. I have learnt about how the Romans mourned and buried each other. There is of course, a specific goddess for it all; Nenia, for mourning and the lamentations sung at funerals. The dead were buried by inhumation or cremation, with burial always accompanied by a funeral. Apparently, they were always placed underground or in a tomb, to shield them from the gods because they had no truck with the deceased. How final this is; how complete a severance.

Burials included grave goods; for the wealthy, vessels full of food and drink, or maybe a gold ring to show their status in the afterlife. The dead held coins in their mouths to pay the boatman to ferry them across. I think of this, and feel the cold clink of money against my teeth.

To avoid pollution (and what a pragmatic combination of the spiritual and prosaic this is), burials had to be outside a town and took place in cemeteries outside the city gates. The only exception to this rule were newborn infants, who were allowed a place inside the walls.

Who decreed this; this is what I want to know. Who decided that this kind of loss merited an exception? A grief that would have gnawed away at a woman as she hurried beyond the city to sit by the grave of a child who had not lived much beyond the womb. In all the rules and rituals, this seems to me to bear a particular kind of wisdom and compassion, that newborn infants should not be placed outside.

In the class tonight, in a way that I could not avoid, I could for a moment feel it all so keenly, so clearly; a woman, her body still baggy from

191

childbirth, walking, head down, her face shielded with some sort of veil. Was it accepted with pragmatism and grace, with an assumption that many infants would not survive the passage into life? Or was it, as I imagine, the keenest of woes, their arms beating their bodies, their hands reluctant to let the small, still form go?

I would like to know more about this, but I think this is enough. The knowledge would cling to me like a damp, yellow fog. I will not think of small, swaddled, still bodies, instead I repeat what I have already asked. Who decided that this was a different kind of loss, who allowed the babies to be kept close by their mothers?

So much of it I see is about wives and mothers, safeguarded by a plethora of gods and goddesses. Men had a genius, which meant begetter, which was perceived as a guardian spirit who helped them to father children. In women, the corresponding spirit was called iuno. Every woman was believed to possess one, a guardian spirit specifically focused on womanhood. There was also Bona Dea, a fertility goddess worshipped only by women, and Terra Mater who was goddess of the productive power of the earth. There was Magna Mater, too, who personified nurturing and protection, and who strode boldly forth with her attendant lions. I like that she was accompanied by broad-pawed lions. I like the thought that she would be defiantly, assertively, just who she wanted to be.

I would like to find my iuno; I think that is what

I am saying. I would like to feel my own enabling spirit; an energy and a confidence which could help me to be somehow different, better. I think that I am a small, hand-tied, worrier. I would like to be more. Is that so much to ask?

Tonight I have learnt about defixio. How can I have lived for so long and never known about these?

A defixio is a curse tablet, a promise to the gods to do something in exchange for action taken against an enemy. It was inscribed on small thin tablets of lead or bronze. The defixio was inscribed with the person's name, and even a desired course of retribution. Afterwards, it was buried, or hidden, or thrown down a well, or fixed to the top of a tree or a post.

How perfect is that? Did the person who wrote it (or had it scribed for them, more likely) walk away with the cool, heavy weight of a curl of lead in their palm, their mind sifting, selecting, where the best place to hide it would be? Perhaps choosing the village well, the lead beginning to collect a thin sheen of sweat from their hand. Or, brow furrowed, trying to nail it into the trunk of an old oak, the knocking of the hammer causing a rush of birds to flap up through the leaves, the echoes ringing through the surrounding trees.

But what I really want to know is whether they walked away purged and cleansed; the lead spinning and dropping down into the well, the twilight gathering around the split oak tree. Was their grievance like a ball of wool knotted inside them, with each step away from the defixio making it unfurl, trail away, until it had unravelled completely, leaving them lighter and free?

And I wonder if Juno read what they requested? Did she dismiss some requests as pure envy, jealousy or spite; some as vindictive even by human standards? But some did she consider, moving her head this way and that, her hand perhaps to her lips while she wondered if this was a just cause indeed. What made her, I wonder, start something in motion?

Wherever the best place for hiding it was, this I know for sure. I know what I would write, I know who I would write. I would drag it out of me like a kidney stone, calcified, thick in my insides. And then, I would wait and see if anything changed. See if I had a space inside me that I could breathe into, fill with air.

Marriage. I knew the classes would get onto that. The first goddess was Cinxia, who looked after the bride's girdle, and ensured that the bride was properly dressed. Ready, I presume, for all that would follow. I like the nod towards the subsequent de-girdling, with all its clumsiness, awkwardness, and half-formed expectations. Then after Cinxia, it is all Juno's domain. She had other epithets, including *Interduca*, which meant she who leads the bride into marriage; *Domiduca*, which meant she who leads the bride into her new home, and also *Lucetia*, which meant bringer of light. She was also *Ossipagina* which meant bone strengthener, or bone setter. There is such wisdom in this – I can think of no equivalent in our times – of a long-married woman being able to call upon a goddess to strengthen her bones. It seems so fitting – for an osteoporitic, post-menopausal woman – to be fortified by a goddess who would strengthen her capacity to endure. In the dog-days of a marriage, before the mutual falli-bility of old age, a boost to continue, when all memory of how it had once been is impossible to summon.

There is another small superstition which appeals to me too, and one which I see has travelled unchanged to our times. The bridal festivities moved from the bride's house to the groom's, and the groom would carry the bride over his threshold to avoid her tripping or stumbling, because if she did, it would be an ill omen for the marriage.

This is so literal as to be something cool and solid I can hold in my hand. How comforting to think that if a bride is deftly carried over the step, the marriage will go swimmingly, bathed in a glow of mutual love. How killing, too, to think that it is jeopardised by a small stumble; a garment edge, perhaps, caught on a rough bit of stone; the atten-dant anxiety on the faces of the onlookers, the sharp intake of breath perhaps by the bride's mother. The feeling that all is spoiled, and that Cardea should not allow the door to be opened.

Tom did not carry me over the threshold. I did

not stumble, I am almost certain of that. I'm sure we carried our bags into the first small house that we rented, after our register office wedding with our parents and a few friends attending. I expect – because this would be in keeping with all that has come after – that Tom would have carried our heaviest bags, and I would have brought up the rear with bits and pieces over-spilling from my arms. I expect we would have kissed each other when we closed the door – a kind kiss, not an unbridled passionate one – or perhaps we did, and I can't remember the possibility.

My marriage has been a kind one and I think this is a good word. I have no knowledge of scalding words thrown across rooms; I have no knowledge of sitting, my knees hunched to my chest, weeping at the slam of a door as he leaves after an argument. He has never sprinkled rose-petals on the bedroom floor, or made love to me until I drowned in an agony of longing. Instead, we lie asleep like two interlocked spoons, my knees tucked into the fold of his; my arm, usually, wrapped around his middle.

Tom is decent and good, and I know this is why I chose him. I knew he would be the kind of man who would always have de-icer for the car on a frosty morning, who would clear the gutters of leaves after the last howling storm of autumn, who would never sit across me at dinner and say, *Don't you think it should be more than this?* I sensed he might feel our life was complete in the way it

196

began, with the two of us, wholly together. When faced with childlessness, I knew he would be supportive, but not intrusive; would not insist on a battery of tests, our entrails held up for doctors to peer at and analyse.

I knew he would like food that I could reliably cook; a soft rice pudding on a cold November night, a thick vegetable soup after a bracing walk on a Saturday, a bowl of strawberries, eaten sitting on the bench in the garden on a warm night in June when the stocks by the kitchen door make the air fragrant and sweet. I knew from the beginning that we would be the kind of couple who push a trolley together around Sainsbury's, discussing whether to try a new kind of salad dressing, or, at Christmas, standing in front of an array of biscuit tins, choosing the one we would most like: We would be small, and quiet, and ordered in all that we did.

I knew he would buy me gifts that were safe and pleasing. A soft woolen scarf, a pair of white slippers, some hand cream infused with the smell of roses. And I would buy him things that would maintain his sense of control, of fastidiousness; a power-washer, so that the car would be clean with wheel hubs shining; a waterproof golf jacket made of correctly breathable fabric; a leather passport holder, a pair of wellingtons with zips up the side.

I knew we would find the same kind of holidays appealing; a barge on the Norfolk broads, sitting next to each other by the wheel, hot mugs of tea in our hands, saying good morning to anyone we passed. I knew we would pore over guidebooks in Europe; go to *duomos* in Italy and remark upon marble and frescoes.

And I knew, most of all, with a clarity that I am still astonished by, that Tom would manage an almost-impossible balancing act, of giving me loving companionship without intruding too close. So, on days when he comes home from work to find me lying on the floor of a room, the curtains drawn, a quick nod to a migraine, he will ask me if he can bring me some tea, or perhaps a painkiller, and with an exquisite sense of superfluousness, will close the door and walk quietly away. I will hear him moving about the house all evening, preparing his supper, perhaps watching the news. And when he comes to bed, he will put his head around the door, ask me if I'm ready to come to bed, and if I say yes, help me back up onto my feet. He will turn away as I rub my stiff joints back into life, and go into our bedroom and turn down my side of the bed. In all these years, he has never asked what demons I am running from, not when at night, I wake sobbing from a dream, not when he finds me standing, my face turned to the wall. Instead, he leaves me, understanding these are things I would not share. Instead, he helps me with all my familiar strategies, poring over a new evening-class schedule, looking for a course that will give me peaceful absorption. Or, after six months, when I change jobs again, helping me decide on a new outlet for my energy.

Tom has helped me to plant an entire border

with Lenten roses, only to re-sow it a month later with a mass of cornflowers. He has done orienteering classes with me, stomping through woodlands with a compass and some directions; sat on a log and laughed with real good humour when we are hopelessly lost. He visited my ailing mother with me every Sunday for years, and has always taken care to ensure that the spoon of sugar in my tea is absolutely level. I cannot bear it too sweet.

He is, I am so vividly aware, a good, good man. Not the kind of man who inspires others to heroic action, or the kind of man who achieves outstanding success. Instead, he is a moderately successful structural engineer, without whom people's house extensions, or new-builds, would not stay upright. He can calculate the load-bearing weight capacity of a beam, and from that, the thickness of the relevant steel. He can tap a wall between rooms, and know if it can be removed or not, and he can quantify the level of insulation needed to conform to government regulations. He uses his digital camera to take pictures of new leading on roofs, ensuring that the drainage is correct and effective. He makes things *sound*, in the workings of his daily life and at weekends he plays golf on a Saturday, and has a drink with his friends.

He makes love to me, and it *is* love, of that I am sure, in a way that is tender and caring, with a slight hesitancy as if I am fragile or something that might break. Sometimes, when he thinks I am asleep, he strokes the side of my face with his hand,

and then rubs his fingertips against his palms, as if conscious of their roughness from his daily work. In turn, I try to do what makes him happy. I chat, I cook, I make sure I am always home first. At Easter, I always buy him a huge chocolate egg. I am not sure, actually, if he likes this or if he eats it to please me. I should ask him, I know, but there are many things better left unasked. I know it would make him uncomfortable after all these years of receiving it; all these years of slightly self-consciously unwrapping the attendant big ribbon.

I have no memory, now I think about it, of robing myself for my marriage. I am aware though of Lucetia and a bringing of light that has been gentle and constant. I am aware, too, that for the most part, we get the marriage we choose. I am grateful to *Ossipagina*, now, for giving strength to my bones. I am mindful of how a childless couple can become fussy, eccentric; visiting farmer's markets to buy only a specific type of honey; having Sunday mornings that become fossilised in their fastidious routine; the ability to predict, absolutely accurately, what each other will choose from a menu and then eating in silence. I have tried to prevent that happening to us.

I am mindful, always, to give thanks for what I have, and to give thanks for our home and the comfort of our existence.

Tonight, we looked at the deities associated with the house. I began the class in a mirthful mood,

200

thinking that our gods, now, would be Dyson or Microsoft, for the power to clean effectively or to e-mail shopping lists for supermarket home delivery. And then, I realised I'd got the wrong end of the stick. For the Romans, it was less about housekeeping and more about the sanctity of the household. Again, the attention to detail, to fine distinction, quite overshadows ours.

We began by looking at the lars, deities who were guardian spirits of the household. Each house kept a shrine to the lars, and they were worshipped at the hearth at specific times of the month. Then there were the penates, who were the gods of the store cupboard. They were the spirits of the pantry or larder. At each meal, a portion was set aside, and then thrown on the flames of the fire in the hearth. Also, the table was always set with a place for them, marked by a saltcellar and a small offering of fruit. On three days each month, they were especially honoured, and the family hearth decorated with fragrant garlands.

This reverence, and thankfulness for food, was matched by homage to fire; to Vesta, the goddess of the hearth. Each day, families made a sacrifice to her, and her feast day was a holiday for bakers and millers. The millstones and asses were garlanded with violets, and hung with small loaves. Vesta also had her own priesthood of women, girls who served her for thirty years. Their hair was fashioned in a style known as six locks, which was otherwise worn only by brides on their wedding day.

As I think about this I am looking at my own small hearth. We have a black enamel woodstove that sits on pale French tiles. I try to imagine what it would be like to throw food into it, to watch it crackle and curl, a charred smell filling the room. I remember the rooms I lived in as a single young woman, with one-bar electric fires and an attendant meter. I think of fake gas fires, with fraudulent flickering displays, and I feel something is lost; that we have lost our reverence for it all. I imagine a donkey garlanded with small fragrant violets, a thick millwheel hung with tiny loaves. I imagine laying the table for myself and Tom, and a third place, with a serving of fruit and salt. I would like to learn more about salt. I'm sure there was a reason that this was chosen. Perhaps for its preserving qualities, for its purification powers. I expect it was thick sea salt, with crystalline edges that pressed into the skin. Would doing this, I wonder, feel like some sort of protective cloak? A mantle around the house, constant thanks for food and warmth.

I have just stood in my small pantry, looking at the rows of food. Tinned tomatoes, tinned tuna, bags of self-raising flour. I have dried herbs that have desiccated to nothingness. I have soy sauce, noodles, bags and bags of pasta. I have a tin of chestnuts that I bought thinking I would find a winter recipe for them; I have puy lentils, cannelloni beans, from my New Year's resolution to eat more pulses. I look at the shelves and think of penates living in here, in habiting this pantry, overseeing all that I make with my hands. I am tempted, ridiculously, to put a handful of salt on the back of the shelf. I have some crystallised ginger, some raisins; would that count as fruit, I wonder? I would like to feel that in here was safe, protected, so that when next I am anxious, I can stand here, faithless, and press the salt into my palm until it marks.

I think I know what I am looking for; I just can't make myself say it yet. Instead, I want to note how much better the Roman version was; how much better than a vacuum cleaner god with no bag to empty. I can see so clearly a family gathered around a hearth; I can feel the delicacy of violets in my hand. I can see a woman weaving her hair into six locks. I can hear the fire spit and crackle as the offering is thrown.

Once, I saw a woman in an upstairs window. She was young, a young face, but with her hair tied back, pulling her skin to her bones. She stood at the window, which was nailed so that it could not be opened properly, and she was banging on the window with the palms of her hands. Her hands banged and smacked at the window; they looked like two crazed birds, fingers splayed, wrists exposed. She seemed to be screaming at a couple who walked away in the street, their heads bowed, their shoulders hunched, against a cold day in March. And the woman was screaming, her words threading like beads into the street, *Don't go . . . don't go* . . . in a voice that was high, razor-pitched;

her voice as if bleeding against the implacable glass. I thought the glass would break, that it would shatter into shards; that the window would rain down in the street, the woman's words interwoven with the slices of glass. But it did not break, instead the window simply misted with her breath. Her face became obscured, her forehead pressed right to the pane. And the couple kept walking, they did not turn around. The man placed his arm protectively around the woman's waist. In the window opposite, a net curtain twitched. A small ignominious twitch, which carried with it the certainty of a life more virtuously lived. I have had a hatred of net curtains since.

Years later, in a supermarket, when I saw a product for keeping them clean and white, I was tempted to knock all the packets to the floor, to watch the white granules sullied by the trolley wheels. And on that day, in that road, with the woman at the window, the *Don't go, don't go* simply fell into the street, onto the daffodils in next door's border, into the gutter where there were wrappers and a coke can. The woman carried on screaming and shouting until she was completely obscured from view. An opaque pane, a searing pain, this is what I saw.

And yet they were my hands against the window-pane that day. My hands that beat and beat against the glass. My hands disturbed the flock of crows in the tree opposite, made them fly up in a swirl of cawing and protesting, their black wings bent back against the cold March wind. The sky was sullen, bruised like an eyelid, and my hands banged and banged, and tried to pull the window open. There were two crooked nails, one inch up from the sill, bent in order to allow the window to open only a fraction. The edge of the nail scratched into my skin; a red bead of blood, the grey, scudding sky, a woman on the pavement, pausing for an instant and then looking at the baby; and the two of them, his arm around her waist, walking purposefully on. I still think I could hear the sound of her heels on the pavement, but I think this is a detail I may have added, to go with the red and the grey and the misting window pane, the sound of my voice which was both of me and not of me; a wailing, a keening, which should rightly have scratched runnels in the glass.

And earlier, six months earlier, aged sixteen, in the kitchen wearing my school uniform, the tunic increasingly tight across my stomach, and my mother drying a Pyrex bowl in her hand, a white bowl, I remember, with a pattern of autumn leaves on the side. My mother, wiping her hands on the tea towel and saying, *What do you mean, pregnant?* as if I'd made the word up myself, or tried it on, like a hat or a pair of shoes.

Beau, I would have called him. Entirely inappropriate I know for a child born in the early 1960s, entirely inappropriate for a child announced in a small, plain kitchen, after a meal of liver and onions. Boo would have been better, for the shock he gave her, but I would have named him Beau, because I knew he would be beautiful. The next day, my mother marched me up to the doctor's, her hand holding tight to my elbow as if I might make a dash for it. My father at breakfast, just looking at me wordlessly, no doubt aware after a conversation whispered across scallop-edged pillowcases.

And the doctor, as I lay on the thin bed and he palpated my abdomen, saying, without malice I think, I am almost entirely sure it was without malice, *You won't of course be keeping it*, and my mother nodding in stark agreement. *I am sure*, she said, *there are appropriate organisations you can put us in contact with.*

For the next five months, I was practically imprisoned in my bedroom. My mother fetching brown envelopes of work from school. *They don't want you there, in this condition, it's a bad example to the others.* In my bedroom, doing trigonometry, drawing the cellular structure of a leaf, declining French verbs with my hand on my belly as it swooped, kicked and dived. I felt so round, so potent, so squashed full of life, my hand able to locate a small, insistent foot. One day, standing naked in front of the mirror, my breasts huge, rosynippled, my stomach blue-veined, pulsing, and my mother walking in, tossing a dressing gown across the room. *Have you no shame? Get some clothes on.* And then she told me that for the last month I was to go to a special home, a place, she said, where there are other girls just like you. Fallen girls, she said, who would have their babies adopted into good homes. They knew just what to do there. It would be taken care of.

Falling girls, I kept thinking, as she left the room; girls like peg dolls with wide, pregnant skirts, falling and spinning like seeds from a tree, their outline distended, their arms stretched out wide. And when I arrived at the home it was to a stern, unsmiling matron. This is what you can expect to happen, she said, running through the process and handing me a packet of looped sanitary towels for afterwards.

The birth, it is still scalding, the hot, spilt blood of the birth. The pain and the fear, and the aloneness, and all the time thinking that he was coming into the world and would not be mine. And the midwife's hands, grabbing and twisting, pushing deep into me to see how far I was dilated. And when I screamed, she slapped me hard on the cheek; *Your mother's outside*, she said. *Behave yourself, you little slut*. And in all this, I thought, no mention of the father, no discussion with my mother, no-one even asked whom. He was just a boy too, a child if I think about it now, seventeen, unsure, his cheek still mostly smooth. The sex stumbled into, discovered, amidst huge swathes of ignorance. I never even told him, and afterwards I learnt that he had moved away. Another thing, I think, probably better left unsaid. The thought of my mother, my father in tow, walking up to his front door, rapping on it sharply with her purple knuckles.

And in labour, wanting so desperately to stand

up, to struggle to my feet, hold onto the rail of the bed, and push like a cow in the field, my body wide ans strong. The midwife saying to me, *Will you just lie down for heaven's sake, will you lie on the bed; you can bite this if you must.* She handed me a gag made of cotton, tied with a sailing knot that was hard to my teeth. All the time I was biting it, I looked at her arm. I'd bite that in preference, I thought, right down to the bone. For months after, vindictively, wishing I'd sunk my teeth right in.

When he was born, he was so completely beautiful, the curve of his lip, his dark hair pressed close to his scalp, his hands and fingers, his tiny nails. I wanted to lick him, to smell him, to nuzzle him up. I said I would feed him, and matron said, *That won't be necessary, we'll just make him a bottle.* But I did feed him, conspiratorially, before she could object; offered my nipple to his mouth and watched him suck, his dark eyes looking intently at mine. A small bead of colostrum gathered at the crease of his lips. I wiped it away with my finger, and stroked the line of his cheek.

My mother came into the room, and sat down on a chair, her face turned away from us both. *Won't you just look at him* I said, *he's beautiful, I knew he would be.* And her face did not turn, it looked intently away. All these years later, I can still draw the geometry of that room. The baby with me in the bed, my mother at right angles to us both. The roundness of my breast, the curve of the baby's face, and my mother's jaw-line, set, her eyes fixed

208

on a white space on the wall. *The most important thing*, she said, *is that he goes to a good home.*

I have tried, with the kindness of age, to interpret her behaviour differently. To understand what it was that would not allow her to look, to scoop us both in her arms and say let's just go home. I can see what happened was common in that age, at that time. I understand that it impeached all her notions of respectability; a well-scrubbed kitchen floor, white washing on the line, no scope for a daughter who was an unmarried mother at sixteen. The knowledge then, as I sat holding my baby all through that first night, that a boy may have fucked me up, but it was my mother who fucked me over. Matron coming into me next morning and saying factually, firmly, *We have found a good home for him, they will come and fetch him the day after tomorrow.* And then, as an afterthought, as she stood by the door (her voice primly factual, her fingers ready to flick off the landing light to conserve electricity), *I'm sure it has been explained to you that it is probably better not to feed him. Your milk will be through and you will have only yourself to blame.*

Two days later, one of the midwives knocked on the door. Can you come down to the Receiving Room, she said, his parents are here. Receiving room, I thought, even now the words scorch my tongue. For what we are about to receive may the Lord make us truly thankful.

The couple were sitting side by side on a couch. I thought they were old, but recognise now they

209

were not. She must have been in her twenties. What did she know about longing at that age?

They were holding hands; I could see a white line on her knuckles. Her face looked calm, composed, but I could not take my eyes off her hand. They were both well dressed; he had on a suit and a gabardine coat. She was small-boned, attractive, wearing a twin-set in pale blue. She looked neat, tidy; her breasts concealed by the fold of her arm. I was aware, suddenly, of my own leaking breasts, the milky patches that had seeped through my blouse. My armpits were sweating, I could sense the white salty rings. My vagina was bleeding, I was sodden between my legs. Before her dry primness, I was a wet, leaking mess, holding my baby in my arms, watching, as in slow motion, the midwife begin to prepare a white cellular blanket.

The matron rattled out his sex, birth date, weight, and asked me to tell any family medical history of note. None, I remember saying, nothing at all, looking at his face while she asked me to hand him to the midwife. Hand him over, like a parcel. Like a bag of potatoes. His small face, now swaddled by the blanket, his fingertips at the rim. Inside, I was screaming *No, no, no*, but in reality, I just stood there, leaking and lost.

The man signed some papers, put the pen back into his gabardine pocket. He put his arm round his wife, who was by now holding the baby, and they walked out of the room. Her eyes did not leave the floor. Matron closed the folder and said

I should go back to my room awhile. Your mother will be here tomorrow to collect you, she said, you can go home soon.

I ran up the stairs, to the bedroom window. The banging and shouting was what happened next. My body shaking violently, blood surging and pulsing. Suddenly, more blood, pouring, until I had to call for the nurse. Another doctor, this time hands pushing, not pulling, trying to push it, slitheringly, all back in. *Your uterus has prolapsed*, he said, failing to meet my eye; *I think it is unlikely there will be any more children*.

Next day, on the bus, swaddled and bandaged, my mother next to me, my forehead pressed to the cool of the bus window. My mother's hands on her handbag straps, her mouth tight, her lips set. Me, ridiculously, looking for the man's gabardine coat. Perhaps they would have bought a pram, perhaps they would be out walking; the knowledge that I knew nothing, not even where in the country they lived.

On the bus, my breasts tight, hot, exploding. My temples pulsing. My nails digging into my palm. When the conductor asked me for the fare, wanting to stand up and shout I have a son, I have a son, and she has made me give him away.

How many times have I thought of him since. How many moments have I imagined what he might be doing now. Wondering if he was crawling, walking, starting to speak. Wondering if he was perhaps riding a bike, balanced with black rubber stabilisers. Wondering if he ran out from school into her arms, his satchel, his lunch bag, dropped onto the floor. I have no hatred for her, despite the feeling that she has stolen my life. It was not her intention, I understand that, she was not to know.

I imagine his life, each tiny detail. Where he has been on holiday, what she has made him for lunch; whether he was well behaved at school, whether he has gone to university. Whether, now, he is married with children of his own.

And Tom knows none of this; I have never breathed a word. When he asked me to marry him, I told him it was unlikely that there would ever be children, and he told me he loved me so much it did not matter at all. And he has been true to his word as friends, work-mates, all had families. I have never felt him look at me, a mournful glance sideways, as he watched a six-year-old struggle to do up a football boot, or held a toddler at a party while the father fetched something from the car. And I hoped, I admit, I cannot say I did not hope, that one day my womb would be filled snug, cradling, like it was. That one day it might surprise me again, and this time let me do it on my own terms. But it didn't. It has stayed slack-lipped and empty, any life within it to spill from it before it has chance to take root.

I never pursued it further because I never wanted Tom to know; my concealment gathering sediment with the accumulation of years. Perhaps a ripple of my mother's shame worming itself into me; snagging itself like a small silver fish hook into my lip, a small, persistent anxiety that perhaps I should have been wiser, cleverer, less predictably inept. Perhaps a thin film of foolishness because I had stumbled into territory that was so run-of-the-mill, as if confirming to myself that I would never amount to much at all. A hot, dry embarrassment as to how I might have appeared that day, so unable to do anything but as I was bidden.

The whole episode so quickly disjointed and fractured from my resumed life. Never spoken of, never alluded to, wiped clean from the slate with a hand that was firm, convincing and resolute, so that sometimes I thought that it was only in my mind, my heart, that it had happened at all.

I did not return to school, but to secretarial college. Rows of faces behind typewriters, girls who had not seen my body as different from their own. Neighbours who never looked sideways, never whispered as I walked by. No, from my physical life it was truly erased; my once swollen belly definitively rubbed away, so that sometimes I lay in bed with my hand on my stomach, wishing for silvery stretch marks that might be a map to show a way back to what once had been. But nothing; my abdomen smooth, unmarked, and taut as a drum skin.

And I compacted it all; layers and layers of compression which made it impossible, when I first fell in love with Tom, to dredge it up from within and say, look there was this also. For so long, mine alone, and impossible to shake this off.

A small fear too, that he might see me as somehow less worthy. A coward, was this what I worried about most? And through all these years, he has never asked, never probed. Has never suggested that our life is not chock-a-block full as it is.

And I have watched other mothers, watched them hold babies, feed them and love them. I have looked into prams and felt myself grow austere, severe, anything to quell the turbulence within. Home to weep, and to lie on the floor of a darkened room. A migraine, a headache, anything except that my heart is still breaking.

And I have nothing to show for it, nothing at all. Except, now, an old womb, which laps only with grief. I was a mother and yet not a mother – how can anyone help me with that? He is my son, yet not mine, he will have no memory of me. I do not even know if he knows the true circumstances of his birth; and yet I am branded with each gram of his skin.

And my mother, towards my mother, how could I be? Watching her smiling with satisfaction when I married Tom. A slow, cold poison that crept through my veins, until I could barely lift my eyes to look at her face.

When she was old, dying, I remember feeding her lunch. The spoon poised by her blue-grey lips, her eyes watery, white-rimmed, half-focused on something beyond me. Her mind, by then, a mishmash of memory and time; the correct event in the wrong context, like snow falling on wet

214

ground. She looked at me, the spoon in my hand, her chin assuming some of its old challenge.

'A baby', she said, 'was there a baby?' she said.

'Would that be mine or yours, mother?' I replied, pushing the spoon into her mouth.

'These carrots are hot,' she said, a glimmer of her old self in her eyes. And in all those years, nothing else said. No allusions in March, when the daffodils come. No mention, in the first five years of my marriage, when I wondered if she was waiting, like a pausing breath, to see if I would stand in her kitchen again, tell her the same words again only this time make it right on her terms. No danger of that.

Women beware women, that is what I thought, and that, in these circumstances, is what my curse tablet would say. It would list them all; my mother, the matron, the midwife, the woman from the adoption services whom I only realised later was in the room. Yet the woman in the twin-set, his mother I suppose I must call her – she is not on the tablet for reasons of which I am still unsure.

Did she become my Edusa, my Adeona; rearing him, loving him, in the absence of a child of her own? If she made him happy, well balanced, how could I bear her ill will? Did she love him and tend him better than I would have been able? I would like to know these things; I think it would bring a kind of peace to my heart.

Whilst she stole him from me, she was not to know that. She took, when offered, the fruit of my

215

womb, and in doing so, pulled out my innards and left me bereft.

And each time I think of it, these events which I must recognise as my life, and my story, my past comes and washes over me and through me. I am, again, before a windowpane in March. Yet, now, somehow, the truth sits candid in my mouth. I think I like my Roman night classes because I like the idea of multiple gods, each one tasked with a sphere of nurture. I am comforted that they might have watched over my son. That while I was not there, he was watched over by forces that were both benevolent and benign.

I am a mother and not a mother, this is the fissure in my heart. Perhaps in recognising this, I can make it whole. I think I should try to reconcile the life I have not lived with the life that I have. I think I should not lie in darkened rooms, but speak the truth, ringingly, clearly. Perhaps, soon, when Tom comes home one night, perhaps I should tell him about the woman-child that I was; a woman capable of conceiving and birthing but not of asserting her will. Perhaps, after all these years of silence, I should tell him that there is a child who was once mine.

Perhaps I should go and stand by my parents' grave; forgive my father for never mentioning it at all. Forgive my mother for doing only what she thought was right; for never alluding to it again, except perhaps in raddled old age. Her silence, perhaps, rooted in delicacy, in not wishing to crack

216

open old wounds, rather than in a harshness that comes from feeling something is done and dusted.

When I went for a walk this afternoon, I was struck by the beauty of the day. The new leaves on the trees were almost impossibly green, and the sky was a plumped-up palette of blues. As I walked, the breeze was soft on my cheek, my blood was quickening, my step light and fast. It became clear to me, suddenly, the singular importance of a life well lived. A life seized, grabbed with both hands, asserted in the face of both what has happened and what is unknown. A life lived not just in spite of, but because of the possibility of awfulness.

Somehow, now, I can see a way that might be different for me. Not a life lived retreating to a darkened room because of something that happened long ago. Not a life lived that is fearful, waiting for another blow to land. Instead, a life that is taken with both hands. A life based on the belief that things can be re-shaped, re-defined, that it is only in death that we lose our power to change. I think I understand, today, on this day when spring is singing around me, I think I finally understand that it is important to be bold.

Perhaps I can compose both a curse tablet and one of reconciliation. Perhaps I can finally acknowledge that this is how it was, for me.

Last night was the final night class on Rome. The tutor brought along some biscuits, some wine, and the class was conducted in a spirit akin to jollity.

We looked at feasts and festivals, at how Romans celebrated and affirmed life.

I am intrigued by the feast of Cerialia, which was predominantly a celebration of agriculture, of harvest. On the last day, foxes were let loose in the Circus Maximus, with burning torches tied to their tails. In drawings of the time, the foxes' tails were taut and tall, the torches blazing boldly around the whole arena. In reality, it must have been different, surely? Wouldn't their tails have been dragged along the ground, their fur singeing and smoking, the foxes scattering in terrified panic? Was there noise, cheering, and the acrid smell of burning, the foxes trying desperately to escape from it all?

We looked at the feast of Floralia too. It began as an agricultural feast, but was appropriated by prostitutes and became their own. A feast of fallen women, a riot of colour and life, hares and goats running, the ground scattered with lupins, vetch and beans.

I can imagine it all so clearly. The firm, ripe blueness of the lupins, the profile of the hares, their long hind legs, their bodies turning, poised, before running madly away. I can see the beans on the ground, self-contained, fatly-round. And all this for fertility, for procreation, for gestation and for blood-rich birth.

A lupin, vetch, a goat with black precise hooves. A hare turning at an impossible angle into the crowd. The tiny, insistent sound of beans tossed upon stone. And all this a shout, a triumph, a tug on life. Like a calf, or a goat-kid, insistently butting its mother's udder as it drinks.

And so, for me today, a new step, a new chance. Today I have contacted the adoption services, and begun the process of trying to contact my son. I have found out that she called him Michael. I hope to learn more, and to face it with strength and equanimity.

Soon, I will tell Tom everything. In a nod to all that has absorbed me, I will lay the table, discreetly, with an extra portion of fruit and a sprinkling of salt. I will put some food on the fire, and watch it sizzle and burn away. I will stand in my pantry and ask the gods of the household to bless this meal.

Michael's adoptive parents must still be alive, but perhaps, just perhaps, there may be room for us. It would be something just to learn what he has done with his life, his life that began in that small, awful room. I want a new memory, not the window in March. I want to be happy about what he started as, and what he became. I want him to know that he was so very loved.

I do not need to think about the past anymore. I think I have heard my iuno as clearly as something called down an avenue of trees. I understand, now, a different notion of womanhood, of motherhood. I can see it as something both uniquely singular and collective. I can comprehend it in a way that makes the fissure in me whole.

I can see Cardea, her hawthorn branch peaceful in her hands. I can see Bona Dea and Magna Mater, her lions sleeping at her feet. I can see a woman carried faultlessly across a threshold. I can see a woman plaiting her hair into six locks. I can see a curse tablet thrown, far and wide, away.

I can see Juno, light-bringing, bone-strengthening. I can see her holding out to me the iuno that is mine. I can feel it pouring into me in a circle, a pulsing, that will not stop. I receive this from her without needing the satiny-certainty of an Evangelical; I need no proof of what I have received. Instead, quietly, triumphantly, I can face myself. I can look into my heart and see that I am more than I was.

I will find Michael and hope that he has room in his life for me. I will tell him how it was, how it has been, and hope that he understands. I hope that his adoptive mother will accept me, that she will understand that she has had the lion's share. I would like to look into her face and obliterate the memory of that long-ago day, her eyes firmly to the floor, the white line on her clasped hand. Her husband efficiently putting the pen back into his raincoat.

In all of this, I will see myself as a mother again. I will reach out, boldly, and share a gift that perhaps can still partly be mine.

CHAPTER 7

The covenant betwixt thee made

When Michael comes home, Sarah is in the garden with the children. Jack is decorating a mud pie with flower heads he has gathered with her, Grace is skipping and singing a song he recognises from his own childhood, and Rory is bowling a tennis ball at a set of stumps, and is talking to himself about it being the final ball of the Ashes. Sarah is cutting sweet peas and collecting them in a basket, and she is looking across at Jack and laughing with him as he walks around his pie, wondering where to place his final head of black-eyed susan.

It makes Michael feel happy (it is as if his chest swells with inhaling it all), and he looks at his family, out in their garden on a Friday night, and he feels it is so solid, so palpable, this sense of their bond, their togetherness. He looks across at Sarah, with her hands full of sweet peas and she smiles at him in the way he has always loved, with a small tilt of her chin, and he thinks that he has never stopped loving her, and that she will always be beautiful to him. Not beauty as it is rendered in magazines, by women who are bone-thin, airbrushed, wrinkle-free but beautiful because her face is still, mostly, as it was when they were young, and the changes are a nod to all their years together, and all the things they have shared, and all the times she has laughed with him, all the times she has chewed her lip in frustration, all the times she has composed her face into what he knows manifests her resolute determination or fury, and he loves her still.

In the kitchen, supper is cooking, but he can tell from the disarray that it will surely be late. This does not matter to him, particularly tonight, because they are all out in the garden and he wants to bottle this moment and keep it in his jacket pocket for ever, and there will be sweet peas on the table, thrown quickly into a jug, and this, he feels, is an acceptable trade-off. For he knows that life will not, and cannot, always be like this; and that he cannot protect his family from a world which seems to him to be increasingly polarised, increasingly intolerant, and from streets which seem awash with the possibility of being stabbed for a mobile or for carrying a briefcase, or having a particular skin colour. And he thinks of all the cases he has done when lives have been macerated by drugs, or crime, or mental illness insufficiently safeguarded, and he sees these possibilities like rusty, crocodile-toothed man-traps hidden in long grass which might suddenly snap shut on his children's limbs and sever them to the bone. And it is because of all this – for Michael is no sentimentalist – that he knows that this moment must be all the more treasured, all the more absorbed into his heart.

'I was thinking,' Sarah says, as she comes towards him on the terrace, 'it would be nice to have a party.'

'A party?' he questions, thinking how she has never lost the ability to surprise him, for her mind to be other than where he expects it to be.

'Yes, a party,' she says, 'in the garden, on a weekend soon. A party with strawberries and Pimm's and summertime food. For our wedding anniversary' she teases, passing him the sweet peas as she does up the lace on her sneaker. 'Do you realise next week we'll have been married for fifteen years?'

She says fifteen as if it's decades and decades, and he laughs and thinks of a motivational seminar they had at the office, where the facilitator underlined the importance of remembering to celebrate what was good, and the idea of a party seems entirely appropriate.

'A party,' he replies, 'that sounds fun.'

And he thinks of earlier in the day when he walked through a park to get to court, and he passed by an orange blossom that was bowed down with thick, sweet flowers. He had stopped for a moment and breathed in the fragrance, and wanted suddenly to break off a huge, great armful and bring it home to Sarah and give it to her wherever he found her in the house, and tell her that he was thinking of her as he paused in the park, and now, as she stands next to him, watching Grace coax a grasshopper into her hands, he wishes that he had taken the orange blossom, even one small sprig, so that the could have given it to her now, his wife of fifteen years. Fifteen years, he thinks, with Sarah always at the centre of his life. He sees her as she was when they were first together, her limbs creamy and supple wrapped around him in bed; he sees her pregnant, her legs tucked neatly like a tailor beneath her, and then with their babies in her arms, her eyes suffused with what seemed like serenity and exhaustion all at once, and he sees her now, and he remembers a psalm at their wedding; *thy wife shall be as a fruitful vine* and he thinks that she is, and he thinks of a pendant he saw in the jeweller's last month, an opal that shone like a shaft of sunlight through sea and he thinks he will buy it for her and give it to her as an anniversary gift. And as he stands there, he suddenly feels ridiculously, ludicrously lucky, to be in love with the woman who is his wife and who has borne him three children. He smiles at the pleasure of standing in his garden on a warm night in May, wishing he had gathered armfuls of orange blossom and brought them to her, and he thinks of the opal pendant and how it will lie on her breast, and that he has never lost the pleasure of watching her sleep.

Jack runs up and asks him to play cricket, and he loosens his tie and rolls up his shirt sleeves, and catches the ball that Rory throws to him, and tells Grace to field out wide by the tree, and he says again to Sarah that a party is a great idea, and wonders if he will ever be able to tell her how much he loves her.

In bed, later, Sarah is awake. She looks at a pale beam of moonlight that has found its way through a crack in the curtain, and she looks at the isosceles triangle it has illuminated on the soft, Turkish rug. The rug looks magical, flyable, as if one could sit on it and go to Arabia, and land by a camel with a harness made of gold and rubies. But she does not want that, she wants to be exactly where she is, and she smiles at her certainty; at her new relief in recognising what it is that they have.

She will arrange their party; she will celebrate their marriage. She will put a marker in the sand and give thanks for what they have shared. She turns and kisses her husband who is only lightly asleep, and he takes her into his arms, and kisses her softly, and the moonlight shines silver on her naked shoulder.

When Sarah picks the post up from the mat the next morning, she automatically sorts it into what is for Michael and what is for her. She notices that an envelope is stamped Social Services but gives it no additional thought. Frequently, additional documents for Michael's work are sent directly home, particularly if they are for a case that begins on Monday.

It is only when Michael (eating breakfast as he opens it), puts down his toast and appears to read it through again, and then goes upstairs to shave, the letter folded in his hand, and the toast uneaten on the plate, and the cappuccino she has made for him untouched on the table, that she wonders if the letter is not what she thought.

When he calls her upstairs, she leaves the children eating their cereal and finds him standing by the basin, the letter open again in his hand.

'It's about my mother,' he says, passing her the letter.

'What do you mean, your mother, I only spoke to her yesterday,' (and now Sarah is perched on the side of the bath and sitting there, the letter in her hand).

'No, not Mum,' he says, like someone who has travelled at a different speed, 'my birth mother, remember – the one you think drives past in a blue car.'

She blushes and wonders what else he has remembered, stored up; what else he will tell her she said with more impact than she gauged at the time.

The letter refers to Michael's birth mother, Judith, and the exceptional circumstances which have allowed Social Services to approach him. The adoption was authorised by Judith's mother because Judith was a minor, and it is this which has meant they are allowed to tell him that she would like to meet. The letter affirms that it is his decision, and that he can choose to pursue the matter no further if he wishes.

'God,' he says, 'this is all a bit unexpected,' and she sees uncertainty in his face, and recognises how rarely it sits there, and she thinks of Sheila and Judith and the notion of two mothers, and he says 'It's not what I thought . . . after all these years. Why now, now with all . . . with all this.' He gestures with his arm, a sweeping motion that takes in Rory's dirty socks strewn on the floor, and Grace's cello and sheet music at the top of the stairs, and Sarah understands that he means that it is not just about him but about all of them; the huge unwieldy mass of all of their lives that might not be able to be fashioned and folded into something for this Judith-mother to assimilate.

'And what about Mum,' he says, 'how is she going to feel about all of this?'

Sarah thinks of Sheila and can picture her so clearly as she will be at this time of the morning, returning home from her night shift as Henry wakes up, making them both a nice cup of tea, and feeding the cat its food on an old Spode saucer, and getting into her sensible nightdress and turning back the cover on their bed, and sleeping until two when Henry will wake her for lunch.

'Talk to her,' she says, 'you may be surprised how she feels.'

Michael goes to the phone by the bed, and speaks to his father. He asks if he can pop round and soon he is gone. Sarah loads the dishwasher and chides Jack to get dressed. She sits at the table and tries to read the paper; she worries about Sheila and what she will think of it all.

Michael stands at the foot of his parents' driveway. It is simple and neat, with space for one car, and there is a blue hydrangea surrounded by a small patch of white gravel. There is a pot of red geraniums on each side of the porch, and on one side of the step two properly washed milk bottles. There is a small index card stuck carefully to the glass outer door, which reads, in his father's clear hand, *no free papers please.*

It is all so safe, so familiar, so utterly known; this even keel which has been the hallmark of his life. This Judith, he wonders, looking down at the letter in his hand, what if she rocks it all to smithereens; what if this Judith-mother makes it all unravel? And yet he knows, as he stands there, that he is glad that she has done this; that seeing her is something he would like to do.

When Sheila answers the door, she kisses him warmly on the cheek. 'How lovely to see you,' she says, and fusses him into the kitchen, plumping up the cushion before he sits down and beginning to make tea. She tells him his father is watering the garden, and he does not answer but instead says, 'I got this today.' He passes her the letter, and she sits down as if her legs are suddenly very old and very tired, and smoothes out the sheet of paper as she holds it on her lap, and reaches for her glasses which are by the side of the washing machine.

As she reads it she thinks of Judith in the mint-green room, also, unexpectedly, of Martha, with her delphinium-blue skin, and although she is reading the letter she is seeing patches of mint, mint and blue. She thinks of Martha in her room and what she said, and of the barefoot girl-mother all those years ago, and she thinks, What a morning this is turning out to be. She looks up from the letter, and looks at the man she has thought of as only her son for so long, and sees in his face something of the uncertainty he had as a child, and she thinks of all the moments she has shared with him, and all the times she cuddled him when he was small enough to fit on her lap, and she thinks that those moments could easily have been Judith's not hers, and understands why this woman should want to see him. And she thinks of everything that preoccupied her last night; Martha, Judith, lives lived, lives not lived. Choices made, things that might have been but were not, and she stands up and kisses Michael and smoothes the hair from his brow, in a gesture she realises that she has not done for years, and remembers how she used to sit on the side of his bed when he could not sleep and smooth the hair from his forehead until his eyes were drowsy with her touch, and she says 'I understand,' and is surprised to find that it is true, and that she means it and that it is said without a sharp wince in her chest.

'I understand,' she says, 'and I would like to meet her too.'

Michael stands and holds her (when did she become this impossibly small?) and this is how Henry finds them when he comes in from watering the garden (for the day will surely be hot, the sky is like a smooth blue sheet). They agree that he will write and say that he would like to meet her, and Michael tells them about the party and Sheila says, 'Why not invite her to that, and then she can meet all of you, and see the children, and see how it all fits.'

When he leaves the house, he calls Sarah on his mobile, and she is so quick to answer he knows that she has been waiting by the phone, and he loves her for this. He tells her that Sheila has given him her blessing, for he realises this was what he was asking of her, there in her cream kitchen, the sound of the sprinkler soft through the window.

'She suggested she comes to the party,' he says, and Sarah feels her heart jump. The party, like a jewelled egg, complex and intricate before her.

On the morning that Isobel phones Kate, Isobel has been up since dawn. She has sat in her garden and watched the sun rise, from a small disc of pearl light to a paint-box of colour.

When Kate picks up the phone she is surprised it is her mother; it is not like her to call early, her propriety usually shrinks from what she would see as an intrusion. Isobel, Kate knows, rises ever earlier with old age; would be out walking the dogs, or preparing lamb shanks to cook for hours in the Aga, and now she listens to her mother's voice as she says, 'I would like to see you, but see you on your own. There is something I need to talk about, there is something you should know.'

She can hear Harry proposing to the children that they all go on a bike ride, and she mouths to him, 'Is it OK if I go and see my mother?'

He asks, 'Is anything wrong?' and she shrugs, the palm of her free hand facing the ceiling, and he says, 'Do you want me to put the bike rack and your bike on the back of your car and you can meet us later at The Plough and we can go for a ride and then have some lunch?'

She nods, and he leaves the kitchen to fetch the bike rack from the garage, and she says, 'Yes' to her mother, 'Yes, I'll be over shortly.'

She puts sun-cream on the children and checks that Drew has cleaned his teeth. She brushes her hair in the mirror, and puts on some lipstick, and wonders what on earth it is that her mother wants to say. Harry comes into the bedroom looking for his sunglasses, and kisses the side of her head as he reaches past her to pick them up from the chest of drawers. 'Why don't you kiss my mouth anymore?' she asks, surprised at her boldness, and he leans over and kisses her mouth; parts her lips with his tongue, and she can smell the citrus of his soap, and taste the mint of his toothpaste, and she touches his hair lightly with her hand, and he rests his hand briefly on her hip. He says, 'See you later,' with a smile, and she can feel a small thawing, a de-frosting, and for a moment she glimpses that there might be a way back.

She listens to her house, alive on a sunny morning in May. Drew comes in to her and asks her to do up his bike helmet. She can hear Oliver taking ice-cubes out of the tray, plinking them onto the kitchen side, and pushing them into their water bottles. Emma appears wearing a different t-shirt from the one she had on at breakfast, and Kate resists telling her this is not a laundry and instead tells her she looks pretty in blue.

When she arrives at her mother's house, Isobel is standing in the driveway, with both of the dogs on a lead, and her walking boots on.

'Have you just got back?' Kate asks, wondering where her mother has been.

'No,' she replies, 'I just can't say what I want to say with all this around me,' and her hand moves in a gesture that includes the house, all its contents, the garden, the old chicken ark. 'I would like to go for a walk,' she says, and Kate nods in agreement, and they go out of the gate and begin to walk along the edge of the field. They take a path that winds around the wheat that is still green and supple. It will then thread through a field that is pale blue with linseed flower. Kate realises that this route will surely end in the churchyard, and wonders why her mother is taking her to her father's grave.

There are early poppies in the headland around the field. The elderflower in the hedgerow is beginning to fatten into lime-coloured berries. Her mother does not speak, and settles into a steady, even pace, and Kate does not speak either, but waits for her mother's cue. For the first time, she does not fill the space with words that are functional, organising. Instead, she lets the silence surf through the wheat and the poppies. Her mother walks on the track beside her, the dogs pulling a little at the prospect of a partridge in the grass.

'I think,' her mother finally says, 'that when you came to see me last week, there was something you didn't say. I think you had something you wanted to say, but decided not to. I know I do not make such things easy, but it is the way that I am. There was something in your face, in your bearing, that was so familiar to me, and I don't want you to repeat mistakes that I have made. I want to tell you something, something I have recently done. There are things you don't know, and in telling you I think it may make things clearer for you.'

She is unrecognisable, this mother who is walking beside her, her words flying from her mouth like small determined birds, as if they have been waiting, storing energy, until this morning, this moment with Kate.

'You should know,' she continues, 'that marriage

can be many things, and that mine and your father's, in its last years, was not what it seemed. Your father both did and did not love me; he loved me in a way that was loyal and decent and kind, in a partnership that stretched for thirty-five years, but he did not love me, he loved another woman called Martha. He met her in a churchyard one May, about four years before he died. I knew about her, I even spoke to her once. Last week, I returned items to her that I should have done years ago; paintings, his diary, things that shone with his love. I would like to have shown them to you, but I wanted to give them to Martha. They tell more eloquently than I can what he shared with her.'

Isobel pauses as she climbs over a small wooden stile. The crop in the field is linseed now, and the pale blue flowers carpet the ground. Kate feels as if her mother's words are snagging into her skin like soft, small burrs. It is as if suddenly her father is back with them again; her father whom she never imagined with a life separate from what they shared. She can feel small sparks of possessiveness, a hot, liquid disbelief, and she cannot stop looking at her mother, seeing her suddenly like a seed case, split open with her secrets spilling out into the field.

'I cannot say it was not my fault too,' Isobel continues,' I can see how I did not communicate, did not share. I think I chose the appearance of love, rather than love itself, and that by the time he met her, he had been unhappy for years. When

234

he met her, it was as if something had fallen into place; I sensed it before I even knew what it was. And I realised that in a way I was more comfortable with that. I found a peace in estrangement which probably explains why it happened. There were moments I found distasteful – I cannot pretend otherwise – the thought that he had sex with her and returned to sleep in our bed; Madeleine Sawyer telling me as we arranged lisianthus in church that she had seen them together at a cathedral in Dorchester.'

(Kate remembers suddenly the florist at her wedding, suggesting lisianthus and roses for an arrangement by the altar, and remembers her mother saying, with a conviction that surprised her at the time, *No, no lisianthus, no lisianthus at all.*)

'When I met her,' Isobel says, 'I was surprised by the kind of woman she was, but when I saw the portraits he painted of her, I realised that was not what he saw at all. I was so small in the face of it all, I think that is what I am trying to say, so dry-boned and parched, where she was ample and warm. She came to his graveside on the day of the funeral; when I walked there in the evening, I found a book she had left for him. I wondered about her grief, about how it was for her. I realised by the end I thought of us as parallel wives, she having part of his life, in truth his heart, and me having his home, his ways, the weight of our history together. She was married too; I do not know if her husband knew, but that is how we

235

lived for those last years of his life, and the pretence, at his funeral, was almost too much to bear. I wept for our marriage, for the loss of him, but also for what I could not acknowledge; that in truth I had lost him many years ago, that the blame belonged to us both, and that I understood why he did what he did. And I am telling you this for all kinds of reasons. Suddenly, concealment sits heavy on my tongue, and I feel that somehow you always thought our marriage was perfect, and if yours is in any way troubled you may compare it to something that did not exist. I am telling you not because I think things cannot be fixed; I could have spoken to your father, I could have asked him to stop. Or, I could have asked him to choose. Instead, I found a comfortable space in the midst of his betrayal, because I saw that I had betrayed him too, because I had not given him my heart.'

'What I want you to know,' Isobel continues, 'is that through all this, he loved you; and that he was bound to us in ways that were also real to him. I want you to know that marriage cannot always be about love, but it can be about other things which can be as valid, as binding.'

They have reached the shade of the church-yard, and are standing by Robert's grave, the headstone now soft with lichen and moss. Kate finds she is weeping; for what she is not sure; for innocence lost, for knowledge, for cameos of harmony shattered, but also for a new truth which sits bone-hard in her chest.

She sees that her mother has faced herself boldly with a clarity that is piercing, and Kate knows instantly that although her mother's account of herself is as someone who failed, in Kate's mind she is valiant, infused with a new kind of bravery, so that suddenly she sees her seated at the piano, perfectly upright and sending measures of scales echoing through the house. She sees that Robert and Martha could have been a catalyst for her world thundering in, the rending of the fabric of her calmly accessorised life. She sees that they taught her that you cannot organise love, but that there is refuge in accomplishment, substance and composure; in index cards which detail how to make chutneys and jams; in a garden which grows more beautiful with each passing year; in a neat hand of bridge, played with relish and grace.

She tells her mother that she has not failed at all; that in her fallibility and her vulnerability she is in fact *more*; that in her acknowledgment of this truth she is more alive than in her endless calm competence. And she holds her mother while her mother quietly weeps, and she looks at her father's grave and thinks that there will be time to think what this changes, but she feels, intuitively, that there is nothing to forgive, nothing to accept save his insistence on living a life with passion.

And Harry, she wonders, how will this influence how she behaves with him, now knowing that her mother's response was mute resignation, and that she will not do this but will tell him what her heart feels. She thinks again of the kiss by the mirror this morning, and the feeling that it may signal a way back to something they have lost.

When Tom comes home, he always looks, as he gets out of the car, to see if any of the curtains are drawn. If not, he checks to see that the house is not in complete darkness, that there is at least one light on to suggest that Judith is in a room that is lit. He looks to see if there is a quick, fleeting view of her by a window, which tells him she has been waiting, intently, for his return. Always this checklist, as he reaches for his bag from the back seat of the car; always the hope that it will be one of her good days.

Recently, however, there have been none of her signs, none of the precursors of one of her small, intermittent collapses. It has been weeks since he came home to find her on the floor with a migraine. Instead, there is about her a new energy, something he is finding hard to place. There is a crackle about her, a fizz that is almost audible. He feels that if she stood close to a match she would burn blue like magnesium.

He is puzzled too, by small incidents he cannot explain. Last night, in the pantry, when he was getting a beer, he found a pile of salt crystals on the shelf opposite from where the salt is kept. It is piled neatly, and kept in place by a small stack of dried apricots and dates. They have been put there recently; they are still soft to his touch, and he wonders why she has done this; why also there is a small sprinkling of violets down by the hearth.

Always he watches her, in a way that is unobtrusive but absorbed. He is always on guard for any small, fast-moving cracks, always watchful for anything that suggests she is beginning to sink. He sees it like scaffolding – how much scaffolding does he oversee each day at work – scaffolding which helps a building remain upright and strong. He loves her, and does not want her to collapse, and so will always be mindful of providing support. He thinks that somewhere in her past she must have been miserable, truly heart sick, and for that he is sorry, sorry that he was not there to make it not happen.

When he walks through the door tonight she is more magnesium than ever. If he did not think it impossible, he would say she almost shines blue. The table is laid (is that an extra place, he wonders, who on earth might be coming?), and he can smell from the kitchen that she has cooked something complex and special.

He goes to wash his hands, and then sits down at the table. He understands there is no time for delay, that she is not interested in small-talk while he reads the paper.

'I have a son,' she says, when he has hardly sat down, and for a moment he thinks she is possibly delusional, and his mind flips back to when they were in their thirties when he would find her crying in the bathroom each time her period started, and he is wondering how to respond when she passes him a letter, and he sees it is from Social Services. It talks about someone called Michael, and then she gives him another letter which seems to have been written by Michael himself, and it explains that he is a solicitor and has a wife called Sarah and three children, and invites them to a party, and Judith is sitting beside him and holding onto his free hand, and she is not crying, she is just looking at him uncertainly and the first thing he can think of to say is, 'a son, a party', and suddenly she is half-laughing and half-crying and her face is close to his and she says, 'I have wanted to tell you for years, but could not find the words,' and suddenly it all makes sense to him. The boys aged about ten she would look at fixedly in the street when first they were married; the teenagers on school trips whose faces she would scan; and she begins to tell him about her mother in a kitchen long long ago, and a birthing house and a matron, and a couple in neat, respectable clothes, and she tells of a baby she has wept about for all of these years, and he holds her while she speaks and as her words tumble into his lap, he can hear the sound of other things falling into place (her face when she looked at her mother with an expression he thought of as barely concealed rage), his wife who has a son, a son who wants to meet them in June.

She stands up when she has finished speaking and brushes her cheeks dry with her hands.

'Are you angry with me for not telling you?' she asks, and he shakes his head and smiles. He observes that her body is not trembling, it is relaxed and still. He thinks that he has not seen her eyes clearer ever. He kisses her and tells her he is happy for them both.

'A party,' he says, 'that beats looking for another evening class,' and she laughs and goes to rescue dinner from the oven. While she is gone he reads again of Michael and Sarah, and thinks that if it goes well it will be like building an extension; a huge new edifice of unruly life grafted onto their small, precise home, and the thought of it uplifts him, because he has his own small sorrows, and he would like to kick a football with a boy and show him how to dovetail a joint of wood.

In the kitchen, Judith is standing in the pantry. She feels as if weights which have oppressed her for years are falling from her chest. She feels bathed in light, her bones feel supple and strong, and she stands in the pantry and scoops the dates and apricots from the shelf into her palm. She goes back into the kitchen and opens wide the window, and throws out the fruit to be eaten by the birds. She reaches down to take supper from the oven. She carries it through to Tom, and tells him she loves him more than he will ever know.

In the bedroom that night, Kate is talking to Harry. She is telling him about Robert, Martha and Isobel, and about her mother's conversation as they stood by her father's grave. As she talks, she sits cross legged on the bed in her pyjamas, and tucks her hair behind her ear, her face focused in concentration. She chooses her words carefully as she builds up the triptych of Martha, Robert and Isobel. She feels somehow responsible for capturing the truth of how it was.

She tells of Martha, and of how her mother met her. She tells of a doorstep in summer, and a woman trapping her finger in the bolt of a door. She tells of a *Guide to English Parish Churches* pushed into the wet soil of a burial mound. She tells of a series of oil paintings that her mother returned last week. She tells of Isobel, today, and her mother's new-found candour and tenacity. She says it was like watching years of truth come spilling from her mouth; truth like an electric current which made new connections, new pictures; a current which destroyed much of what she thought had been. She speaks of her father, and of the choices he made. She says she will feel, in time, bereft, that something which meant so much to him he kept secret from her, but she knows also that he behaved as any parent would, in protecting her from the fact that he did not love her mother. She is cautious in how she describes Martha's and Robert's relationship; both because she realises much of what Isobel knows is gleaned from his diary and also because she is sensitive to the fact that Harry has never known Robert. She does not want it to appear like an affair characteristic of a lusty old dotage. It is important to her that Harry sees it has some kind of valour, although she wonders whether this is for her father's sake or her own. She wants him to understand that it was a connexion that Robert and Martha could not ignore, although she wants him to see that there are other ties that bind.

As Harry listens, it is hard for him not to see it as a story she is telling him; a long ago church altar woven with ivy and lisianthus. A woman on a beach painted with an iron in her hand. A series of paintings, tied with beautiful flat knots and kept in a cupboard for years. He has only known Isobel as a widow, so has only known her alone, and so her isolation, her dignity, her refuge in accomplishment are familiar to him. His knowledge of Robert is composed of old faded photos; a drawing of a frog; his almost empty study which bears little resemblance to how it was when he was alive. He has held his father-in-law's trout rod, and felt the groove where he must have worried at it with his thumb, but this is the only insight he has of him as animate and alive.

When she pauses in what she is saying (and he is unsure how she wants him to respond) he notes that these incidence confirm that we are always in essence alone. The drama of Kate's childhood, Kate's adolescence, re-configured, re-drawn, cannot be something that he feels as viscerally as she.

Then, her mood changes, and she lifts her eyes to look him full in the face. She has been thinking, she says, of how she would feel if she were her mother. How she would feel and react, if he were to find love elsewhere. Kate tells him that she still loves him, loves him as she did on the day they were married, but that it is not enough to love without being loved in return. She wants to know, she says, if he does still love her, and tells him that if he does not, she would prefer to be alone. She will not live, she says, like her mother chose to do, her husband's heart elsewhere, her mouth crammed with a parchment of lies. She will not compensate loss by strapping on an armour of accomplishments.

'I want to know,' she says directly, 'how your heart feels.'

She tells him that lately she has considered that he might be having an affair, or if not an affair that his gaze has been drawn elsewhere.

'I do not want to know if you were tempted,' she says 'I just want to know if anything happened. I need our relationship to be built on truth.'

He looks at her body across from him on the bed. He remembers how when they were first together she used to sit like this and talk to him at night, and he is suddenly painfully aware of all her complexity, her textures, and he sees that for a number of years he has taken her for granted, like something familiar kept in a coat pocket. He sees their marriage landscaped, a series of negotiations and compromises. Lines drawn and re-drawn, under an accumulation of children and change. He understands, suddenly, the validity of small triumphs, small miseries. He understands, now, with an impact that winds him, the accumulated truth that comes from the relentlessness of facing each other each day.

'Nothing has happened,' he says, and he is enormously glad it is the truth; glad that Sarah in the meadow said, *We must not*. He wonders, briefly, if women have more emotional insight, more emotional literacy than men; how it is only really now that he can see the whole context for himself.

'I think I was working something through,' he says, and he knows it sounds feeble, lame, paltry on the bed between them, when his wife seems, on this night, to be glowing with certainty, conviction. She looks at him and does not speak, as if waiting for him to say more.

'I do not want to leave you,' he says,' I love you, and I am sorry if I have hurt you.'

He takes her in his arms and kisses her like he has not done in months, and his wife's body feels to him to be infinitely precious and fragile.

Later, as she lies sleeping, he watches her face as she sleeps. He traces her cheekbone to her lips and thinks how close he came to jeopardising all that he has. He can hear Oliver murmuring in his sleep, and the showerhead in the bathroom that is dripping softly. The breeze is picking up outside and he can hear the drainpipe beginning to tap against the wall. Tomorrow he will climb the ladder and make it secure. He will make blueberry pancakes for his wife and bring them to her for breakfast in bed. He will play Monopoly with his children and let Drew have extra money from the bank. He will make love to his wife again because he had forgotten how good it could feel.

He is filled, suddenly, with a warm, defiant pride. He thinks of life, of the possibility of other lives lived and is filled with a gratitude for this one, this life chosen and lived with Kate and their children. He settles into the pillow, and kisses his wife's mouth as she momentarily stirs. He reaches over to her hand, and holds it as she sleeps.

Sarah wakes. It is the day of the party. Last night, she sat on Grace's bed as Grace fell asleep, and answered her questions about who was coming, what food would be served, and told her yes, she could help hand round the canapés, and carry the tray with the glasses of Pimm's.

Sarah has not told her about Judith; she does not want her to be fizzing with a weight of expectation. She knows she would be full of questions, and want to know how it all happened. How will it be for her children, she wonders, the notion of suddenly having three grandmothers (she feels strongly, protectively, that she does not want Sheila pushed aside).

The more the merrier, her own mother had said, phoning her before she left to go on holiday to Corsica. *I can't believe I shall be missing it*, she said of the party, *especially now when there is all that drama to unfold. I wonder what she looks like, I wonder how she will greet Michael. Darling,* she concludes, *you must memorise every detail for me. I shall need to know it all upon my return.* At the end of the call, she laughs and says, *Think yourself lucky, imagine having two of me,* and Sarah tells her to text that she has arrived safely, and puts down the phone and is struck by how her mother can always achieve perspective by seeing everything as if it might be performed on stage as a play.

Sarah rolls over in bed and puts her head on Michael's shoulder. She senses that he has been awake for a while but is only now ready to talk.

'Are you nervous?' she asks.

'No, just curious,' he says, 'although I am glad there will be other people here, to cover the silence if it's disastrous, if she looks at me and feels no connexion at all.'

'That won't happen' she says, 'she would not have tried to find you if she felt no connexion. I think it must be strange though; I wonder how physical her memory is of you, or if your birth is something that feels as if it happened to someone else. She was so young, I can hardly imagine how it must have felt.'

'I'm curious,' Michael repeats, 'I did not realise how curious I am.'

Sarah gets up and dresses and drinks coffee as she makes a list. The caterers are bringing the food at eleven, and she needs to pick up baguettes and collect the flowers. She loves collecting flowers – it always seems so indulgent, so special, and even if she is only wearing jeans and a t-shirt, she knows she will feel part of a world that is more beautiful, more elegant, as she carries black buckets to the car that stand tall with lupins and delphiniums, and stems of willow and eucalyptus, and bold, white daisies. She will feel as if she might be wearing leather gloves buttoned to the elbow, and a jaunty hat with a perfectly turned brim. She shakes her head at her own folly, but the luxury of it clings to her for an instant. She tips the remnants of her coffee into the sink, and calls to Grace to hurry if she still wants to come.

She goes out into the garden and looks at the trestle tables stacked against the wall. There is a stillness in the air that promises heat to come. It will be a beautiful day, she knows this in her heart. It will not rain at her party, she is certain of this.

Michael has mown the grass, and she has planted some pots with geraniums and Indian mint. She imagines all their guests, gathered here from noon, and the garden seems pregnant, quietly waiting for it all. And she wonders if sometimes there is a tide, a momentum that is invisible to our purposes; a scheme to the order of things which takes years to fall into place. (She thinks of this party which was meant to be an affirmation of her marriage with Michael, and sees how subtly it has transposed into not being about them at all. Instead, she understands it is a context for Sheila, Judith and Michael; an occasion through which Judith might finally meet her son. And she wonders what sequence of events prompted Judith to try to find him; what Michael was doing at the moment when Judith first telephoned the adoption services.)

She thinks of this momentum as a breeze, invisible to the eye, which carries things forwards, by years, decades, into contexts unimaginable at the time of their beginnings. She thinks of Judith and imagines what she must have felt being forced to give up her son (she sees her own babies in her arms again and cannot imagine how it would have been to hand them over to a stranger). She imagines pain being blown up-wind like a blood-red seed, to be dispersed and assuaged in a garden in June, where Grace is running towards the car in the driveway, her half-eaten toast in her hand, her hair streaming behind her.

She wonders if Sheila is nervous and how it will be for her. She imagines Judith laying out different outfits on the bed, and wondering how to appear, how to seem, when she first sees her son. She thinks about what it means to be a mother, and what mothering is, and knows that she sees Sheila and Judith as mothers to him both. She holds her hand out to Grace and helps her scoop her hair up into a scrunchy. She unlocks the car and says, 'Come on, we will be late picking up the flowers.'

*　　*　　*

She could have called him Beau, Judith sees that instantly as she walks into the garden with Tom, and although she is nervous she is also poised, her mind working at full speed. And she thinks, *Yes, he could have been Beau* because he is a tall, good-looking man, and at that moment he is greeting some of the other guests and he does it in a way that is warm and confident, and she sees a woman beside him whom she guesses to be Sarah, and there are a number of children flying around like butterflies whom she cannot place or name, but she looks at it all and it looks so lovely, so full of life, and she can imagine Sarah in Sainsbury's with a trolley overflowing with shopping like women she has seen, and it all conveys an image of family that she finds uplifting and joyful, and she smiles at Tom, and he squeezes her hand as Sarah comes forward to greet her.

She is like Grace, or rather Grace is like her. Sarah is stunned by this as she puts her arms out to Judith. The line of her forehead, the way her hair tucks behind her ear, how astonishing this is, Judith's resemblance to her grandchild. She thinks of Judith's DNA, tucked within Michael's. She thinks of Grace, growing inside her own womb, and there she is, coined just her like grandmother. Sarah thinks of connexions, about who is connected to whom; blood-ties, love-ties, like a net that holds them suspended yet animate together. Judith introduces Tom, and Sarah instantly likes him, and Jack runs up and tells her that his plane is broken and Tom asks him if he can look at it and says, 'I think we can fix that.' She looks at Judith and says, 'I am so glad you came,' and thinks that she has never spoken more truthfully in her life.

Michael looks and sees Sarah talking to Judith (what will he call her, he wonders, and decides that he will avoid saying her name. To call her Judith would be too obviously to avoid the alternative). Two mothers, he thinks, almost letting himself smile; what a thing for a man to discover at forty-one (no mid-life crisis, he thinks, from a lack of attention). He looks at Judith and tries to decide how he would perceive her if she walked into his office as a client. She is tall, strong-boned and her hair is cut in a bob. Her eyes are quick, alert; he senses that she is taking everything in. She looks nice, he concludes, and recalls that she was only six years older than Grace when she gave birth to him. She has had no other children; he is surprised to find that as something of a relief. As an only child, he thinks he would find having new siblings more complicated, although he wonders how that emptiness might have been for her. He looks across at Sarah and wonders how she has the ease to talk without the least trace of self-consciousness, as if she had talked to Judith every day of the week for years. He feels there are so many big things that he wants to ask, to say; questions like boulders to be inched round on a narrow path. He will not talk to her yet; he feels flustered, unsure. He can see that his mother is crossing the lawn in Judith's direction. It seems appropriate that they talk first, he decides, and busies himself checking that enough wine is opened.

He recalls that when he was a child, and Sheila told him he was adopted, she told him his birth mother had given her the gift of her life. She told him her life would have been one she could not recognise as her own if she had not been a mother, and he understands that Sheila feels gratitude to Judith, and some union for something shared, although he is not sure what this is. 'On the day we collected you' she once said, but then could not speak further.

Judith and Sheila recognise each other without introduction, and as both step forward, it is impossible to say who moves first, and both seem uncertain what to do with their hands. They are both struck that they look older, they have different skin, different hair. It is odd to look at each other and be aware of their younger selves inside; like a kernel inside a shell, this is how Judith sees it, her memory of Sheila inside the casing of her sixty-something self. There is a residual embarrassment (on that day in the Receiving Room, Judith standing while Sheila sat, and Sheila puzzled as to why they had not given Judith a chair). They are intimately connected strangers, this is how Judith understands them, and she resists the temptation to take Sheila's hands in hers.

'Wasn't that place terrible?' Sheila says, because she feels that any attempt at small talk and platitudes would be ridiculous in the circumstances. 'All those girls, all those babies, it was not right, really, the way it was done.'

'It would be different now,' Judith replies, 'there is no shame to it now,' and for a moment they are silent, united in the memory of that room. A question of timing, Judith thinks, twenty years later and it would not have created a ripple, but instead she says 'I can still picture the two piece suit you wore.'

'I did not understand why your feet were bare,' Sheila says. 'Years later, nursing, always insisting that people had something on their feet.'

'That matron,' says Judith, 'she must have been close to our age now. I wonder how many babies she had handed over like parcels.'

'Like parcels, yes, like parcels,' Sheila assents, yet remembers how it felt as if all her Christmases had come at once. She pauses, and can no longer bring herself to look Judith in the eye.

'The window,' she says, 'I heard you at the window as we walked away down the street. I could not turn round. I am sorry. I could not turn round.'

And Judith bites at her bottom lip, a small moment of letting go. She is glad that the window pane did not break, that her hands do not bear any visible scars.

'I have loved him,' Sheila says, 'I could not have

loved him more. I did not take it lightly, I can promise you that.'

Judith can see that Sheila is decent and good. She thinks that she was, indeed, her Adeona, her Edusa. She brought up her son when it was deemed that she herself could not, and she feels a debt of profound gratitude when she expected only to have felt a lack of ease.

'He is lovely,' Sheila says, 'as we are both his mothers I think we are allowed to say that. You will be very proud of him, when you see how he is.'

Judith nods, for suddenly it is difficult to speak, she is seeing so clearly a notion of motherhood shared, of an iuno that is strung between herself and this small, round woman.

'And the children,' says Sheila, 'oh how you will love the children,' and Judith can see, for reasons she cannot yet understand, that Sheila is holding their lives out to her and inviting her to share. It is more than she could have hoped for and she feels possibility surge through her chest. Like a slide cast up from a projector, she sees the Receiving Room. She sees her own dampness, and thinks of the woman who wrote quietly all the time in the corner behind a desk. She sees Henry and his pen, and the white cellular blanket, and then all of it evaporates to this, to this now. She looks at Michael's and Sarah's garden on this day in June, at Sheila's face which is older, softer, and is nurturing and warm. She looks at the sky which is impossibly blue, and is aware of a child on her right, offering her a glass of Pimm's.

'This is Grace, Michael's daughter,' Sheila says, and Judith looks down at the child's hand on the side of the tray, and she sees with a start that it is a smaller, mirror image of her own, with the same shape of thumb nail, and the same broad finger tips. She smiles at her granddaughter, who does not know that she is that, and says, 'That would be lovely, thank you,' and lightly touches her hand as she takes a glass, and all of it, everything she can see, crystallises into a picture in a myriad of colours, and she feels it settle and establish itself with a flourish right in her heart. She turns to Tom, and he thinks she is more radiant than she has ever been in her life.

Isobel smiles warmly at Sheila as she approaches – Kate has told her about Judith – and Isobel cannot imagine that this has been easy for her. But Sheila looks calm and happy, Isobel is struck by this, and seems entirely natural and relaxed as she walks towards her, pausing to kiss her grandson as he runs by holding a small wooden plane. Isobel wonders what it would be like to feel your child both was and was not your own. She knows how this feels in relation to a husband, but she thinks it must not be the same with a child and a birth mother. Would the notion of that original connexion be intimidating, she wonders, the anxiety that a mass of similarities and shared insights might suddenly fall into place? Would it diminish all the years of providing, cooking food, tucking into bed, or would that seem solid, massive, in the face of a blood tie that is severed at birth? Sheila looks serene, this is all Isobel is sure of, and she is impressed by her dignity, and she kisses her cheek with real warmth.

'How are you?' says Sheila. (She is beginning to think that she can take all this in her stride. She is enjoying the party, she is glad she has spoken to Judith; she feels in her own mind a sense of resolution, of something that is complete.)

'I'm well, thank you,' says Isobel 'I'm trying to ignore any complaints my old bones make,' and Sheila assumes the face of a geriatric nurse, and says, 'You should see some of my patients, and you would know your bones don't count as old, although I saw something last week that should cheer us all up.'

'What?' says Isobel, for she has not seen it coming; she knows that Sheila is a nurse, but does not know where she works.

'Some paintings,' says Sheila, 'of a woman who must have been in her sixties when they were done, and they are lovely, unusual, but lovely all the same. The woman looked beautiful, and so full of life, that's what they make me think, and I shall think it next time my knees creak when I get out of bed.'

'Is her name Martha?' asks Isobel, who decides

that the only way on is forward, and Sheila says, 'Yes, how on earth did you know that?'

'My husband knew her, not me,' Isobel replies, 'it was he who painted the portraits. They were lovers right up to the time that he died.'

She has said it; she has said it; it has fallen like a cherry from her lips.

How casual, how powerless, it sounds, she thinks, when it is said like that. How much easier it is to breathe, she observes, when one is jettisoned of untruth. She breathes to the bottom of her lungs, and thinks that it is cleaner this way.

She sees that Sheila is hesitating and is unsure how to respond. (Is it tactless, Isobel wonders, the style of her new-found forthrightness? It is not good manners, she knows, to make a person feel uncomfortable, however personally unburdening it might be for her.)

'It's all right,' Isobel says quickly,' surprising, but all right. The older I get the more I realise that marriages are not always what they seem.'

And Sheila's eyes connect with hers in a way that is unexpected, direct, and she says, 'I know,' with a complicity that hints at knowledge, and at some sort of kinship.

'But,' Sheila continues,' the most obvious connexion is not always the only measure,' and Isobel finds she agrees, and would like to ask her to say more, but old habits die hard and she allows herself just one small sliver of reticence.

'Look at us,' Sheila says, 'two mothers for one boy; two women for one man long-dead. Life isn't always neat, we shouldn't expect it to be so.'

Isobel smiles at their wisdom long won.

Sarah is standing by the barbecue when Harry approaches.

'Happy anniversary. You look lovely,' he says, taking in her blue crinkle-silk dress and the opal pendant that gleams on her skin, and he hopes for a time when he can look at her without desire, when she will no longer represent something that could never be his. And although Sarah can feel a small residual pulsing, a tiny arching of the smallest vertebrae of her spine as if part of her body is invisibly strung to his, she knows that it will ebb, gradually, like the tide as it withdraws from the shoreline, and that with patience she will find herself able to look at him without longing, because her eye will fasten on to everything else that she values and she will be peaceful, she knows this in her heart.

'And so do you,' Sarah smiles, and they both feel that what they have said is almost without heat, almost without fervour, as if a thermostat has been turned down which will allow them, soon, to interact as friends again.

'You were right,' Harry says, 'thank you for seeing it better than me,' and she smiles and thinks of all the things they will not do, all the knowledge of him that she will not have, and she feels the possibility of it begin to leave her body like an exhaled sigh.

She remembers suddenly a phrase her grandmother used to say; *hold a candle*, was it? *Holding a candle for someone*. And she likes the image, with its small halo of religious sanctity, a candle held, soft and flickering in the palm of one's hand. It is a candle also, she reflects, which marks that someone as special, not in a way that is manifest or distinguished by particular behaviour, but in a feeling gently treasured, kept safe from harm. Such a candle, she thinks, can burn alongside all that is greater, all that has the greater claim. She sees what she feels for Harry as a detail on the border of a canvas that is filled with Michael and the children. She is peaceful with this, and she smiles as he says, 'Kate and I have been talking; we are in a better place,' and she leans over and kisses his cheek in a way that is almost entirely without desire, 'We are lucky' she says, and he agrees that they are.

Later, she sees him and Kate talking to a couple from Michael's office, and she sees that his arm is resting around the scoop of Kate's spine. She is happy at this; her party feels as if it is somehow mending and healing, and she walks up behind Michael and places her arms around his waist. 'Happy anniversary, darling,' she whispers into his ear.

When Michael finally stands before her, it is almost audible for Judith, the shattering of old images, tumbling in her mind. *You are so grown* she wants to say, but realises this is ridiculously obvious. She thinks of the image she had of him as a small boy, eating his lunch and going out to play; she thinks of the bike she imagined him riding, his face in school photographs, the bride that she fashioned for him, and none of it, she thinks brightly, is as perfect as this, as he raises his arms, palms to the sky, smiles and says, 'Well, I hope I'm not going to be a disappointment.'

And she laughs with real pleasure – how unexpected this is – that the first thing he says should be so easy to respond to.

'Likewise,' she says, and he sees there are things they will share.

He gestures with his arm – Sarah, all of the children, the house, the dog asleep under the tree – and he says, 'I think it will perhaps be like getting on board a roundabout that is moving,' and she replies, 'I would like that,' and he leans forward and kisses her cheek.

Later, she is sitting on a bench and talking to Henry, who is mild and gentle, but speaks with pride of all that Michael has achieved. It is warm in the sun, and she can see that he would like to sleep, and so she leaves him in the dappled shade and stands at the edge of the lawn.

She looks at all the women at the party (there is someone pregnant, there is another holding a little girl by her upstretched arms as the child paddles her bare feet in the grass). They are all

Juno's women – she sees them vividly as that – as Sarah bends down to Rory who is showing her an enormous snail; as Kate re-ties a bow in Emma's hair; as Isobel explains to Oliver how to graft one plant onto another. She sees Sheila sitting beneath the apple tree with Jack cuddled on her lap. She thinks of maternal love, and its insistent, primordial primacy and energy, and she turns to find Grace by her side, holding up a huge bowl of strawberries, and she looks down at her hands and feels they are overflowing with blessings that will fly up beyond her like small, white doves.

She picks up a strawberry with her finger and thumb, and the strawberry is perfect, plump to the touch. She can smell its sweetness, and see a small patch of juice on her finger. If ever there was a perfect strawberry, she thinks, this has to be it. And she thinks of a stone thrown into a cool, clear lake, and concentric ripples which echo its perfect symmetry, and she knows that if she looks up (for her eyes suddenly have tears in them and she knows the blue sky will turn to mist), she knows that she will see each atom of this garden, and each person in it, as an amplification of what she holds in her hand.

There are times in life, she knows, when everything is dysfunctional; when the idea of a clean connexion, a streamlined flow of nerves and synapses, seems impossible in the face of obstruction, blockage. There are times, she knows, when anxiety can suck the breath from the lungs, when

261

the only way to persevere is with a firm clench of the jaw.

But there are times, she thinks (and now, as she places the strawberry into her mouth, she looks for Tom and sees that he has been encouraged to play football with the boys, and sees her son across the lawn and feels such joy) there are times when we are collectively redeemed, and it is so, today, and she gives thanks, for it will always be enough.

ACKNOWLEDGEMENTS

Martha's ecclesiastical knowledge owes much to Simon Jenkins' wonderful book, *England's Thousand Best Churches*; Judith's knowledge of Roman gods to L. and R. Adkins' comprehensive *Dictionary of Roman Religion*.

For support and encouragement my thanks to Freda Blackwood, Jane and Bronek Masojada, Mark Daugherty, Corinne Hayes, Abha Joshi-Ghani, Maeve Quaid, Beaty Rubens, Sally and Jeremy Rowlands, Faith Stevenson, and Tess Wicksteed.

I would like to thank everyone at Transita, especially Giles Lewis and Nikki Read, for their vote of confidence, and my editor, Elspeth Sinclair, for her judicious input.

I am indebted to my agent, Helenka Fuglewicz, for her zest and grace, and for making everything seem so possible, and to both Ros Edwards and Julia Forrest at Edwards Fuglewicz for helping to make everything happen.

Claire Batten, Barbara Bradshaw, and Linda Longshaw have been there at each step of the way, and generous with their insight, wisdom, and time. Heartfelt thanks.

To my parents, Edwin and Jean Langdale, love and gratitude for their willingness to applaud and support whatever the endeavour; and to my sister, Rachel, for perspective always.

To my children, Finn, Georgia, Harry and Noah, huge love for the insights they have given. And finally, enduring love and thanks to Hamish, for lending support and sustenance in his own inimitable fashion.